MEDIA F.ABLE

WRITER:
MZ HOLME
EDITOR:
AHLIA WATSON
CONTRIBUTOR:
GAZ NEPTEWN

BELFAST - NORTHERN IRELAND - NAYVAYAH - 2021

CHILDREN'S STORIES FOR ADULTS

MZ HOLME

All these stories
have been transcribed
from recently discovered
cassette tapes.

Scarlett

Scarlett was a 12 year-old girl, on the edge of becoming a woman. She had a freckled face and brown hair, cut into a long bob.

Scarlett's childhood was happy, up until her father died. After the tragedy, her mother moved her and her little brother and sister to a new house.

It was not the same as their old house. Scarlett found it ugly, so she stayed in her bedroom reading books and eating chocolate bars, hidden in her bedside cabinet.

One morning she woke up and went down for breakfast, but she could not find her family anywhere. Maybe they had gone out, they should be back later, she thought.

So, Scarlett when back to her bedroom to read.

Lunchtime came and still the family had not returned. Scarlett grew frightened but thought it best to wait. Then at dinnertime she walked to the kitchen again, but still no sign of her family. Scarlett did not know what to do, so she ran to her bedroom, pulled her bedsheets over her head, and cried herself to sleep.

When she awoke in the morning, for a brief moment she had forgotten about her missing family. Then it dawned on her, and a feeling of deep sadness grew in her tummy.

She wanted to wish that her family where downstairs, but the sadness inside her told her if she wished for anything good, only bad would happen. Scarlett was afraid to do anything now, in case something bad happened. Was it her fault her family had left? She pondered.

Pushing the thought away, the sadness engulfed her. She climbed into bed and vowed to not leave it until her family returned. Scarlett waited seven days, and they still did not come home.

Not once leaving her bedroom, she survived on one chocolate bar a day, from her bedside cabinet.

On that seventh night, she had a dream. A man with a large beard, long hair and a tall hat was standing by her bed talking to her.

Scarlett, I've come to help you, he said. But you must leave your bedroom first thing in the morning, or my help will not reach you. Please be brave. There is nothing to be afraid of.

Scarlett awoke with a fright. Who was this strange man talking to her in her dream. Slowly she fell back to sleep. That morning, she heeded the strange man's instructions and left her bedroom.

The house was deadly quiet, except for the sound of her heartbeat in her ears. As she walked down the hallway, she noticed the wall paper dripping all of its colour away. It ran down the walls, leaving old grey brick work exposed.

Terrified, she ran down the stairs, but her feet sunk into them, up to her knees like slime. She pulled herself out and ran back to her bedroom, slamming the door. But this was not her bedroom. It was a room she had never seen. It was old and decrepit.

She saw another door and ran to it, entering into another room she had never seen before. The sadness inside her swept outwards, and she collapsed on the floor trembling. As she lay hugging her knees to her chest, she shuddered herself to sleep.

That night the man came to her in a dream again.

You are so brave for leaving your bedroom Scarlett, he said.

But it was horrifying, why did you make me do that, she said with anger.

Because you cannot be afraid of the house you live in Scarlett. As scary as it might seem, you must not be afraid of it. I am sorry, but I had to frighten you, for you not to be afraid, he answered.

But it's not the house I live in. It's rotten and crumbling and mouldy and old, she cried.

You may not understand this Scarlett, but it is your own fear that is making the house like this. Remember before your father died? Your house was perfect but then you moved and this new house was ugly to you. And one day you woke up and you were all alone, your family were gone.

And I miss them so much, Scarlett wept.

I'm going to help you get out of this house, but you must listen carefully to what I'm going to say, the man consoled her. Tomorrow night when you fall asleep, you need to make yourself appear in my dream.

How on earth I'm a going to do that, Scarlett snapped, I have no control over what I dream. Oh, you do, said the man. Now, listen very carefully. Tomorrow night as you fall asleep, I want you to listen to the beat of your heart. Your heart knows what's best for you and will never deceive you. Then, as you drift off to sleep, I want you to say to yourself, three times: I Was Free. I Was Free. I Was Free.
Then, let the beat of your heart send you to sleep. From there, you will have to do the rest yourself. If it has worked, you'll be standing beside my bed, as I sleep. Gently squeeze my hand, and we'll be awake in my dream together. Only then can I get you out off this house.

Scarlett was exasperated: Why can you just not get me out of this house in my dream. Here and now. Just get me out.

I hold no fear in my dreams, the man said, only love. Your dreams have been built on fear, and only love can set you free from that fear. You have not known enough love in your life to set you free from fear. But I have. And after you are free, you will too.

Scarlett awoke with a gasp. She sat up like a dart. The room around her was dark. The walls seemed to be breathing.

I don't know what's real any more, Scarlett cried to herself. She slowly stood up like a dog that had been beaten. Her joints ached and creaked just like the house.

Numb from the horrors of what had become of her life, she walked from room to room like a zombie. The rooms shifted and changed, like an unending moving mosaic of a nightmare.

She walked up and down stairs that led nowhere. Through doors that led to more doors. Empty rooms that led to empty rooms. Wallpaper peeled. Wooden floors creaked and splintered. Water dropped from the sagging damp ceiling. The stench of mould and rot filled the air.

Scarlett couldn't even find her own bedroom. Everything of comfort had been taken from her. She sat in the middle of a dilapidated room, her head in her hands. She felt as empty and as old as this house was.

Then, she remembered the good times with her family. The beautiful food her mother would make. How funny her little brother was. How protective her little sister was, even though Scarlett was the eldest.

A teardrop fell from her right eye. She imagined that teardrop contained every happy memory she had ever had. She let it run down her face without wiping it away.

She grew tried and curled up like a baby in the womb. Suddenly she remembered her dream, the words echoed in her head: Tomorrow night as you're falling asleep I want you to listen to the beat of your heart. Your heart knows what's best for you and will never deceive you.

She listened to the quiet thump of her heart. The more she listened the heavier it thumped. She could feel it pumping blood to her entire body as it reverberated in her chest. I Was Free, she said to herself. I Was Free. I Was Free.

Darkness descended as she drifted off...

Her eyes opened. She was wide awake, but her body was asleep. Her eyes darted around the room, but she could not move. She was paralysed, and when she tried to speak her mouth wouldn't work, only slurred elongated sounds oozed forth.

She put all her effort into moving her forefinger, but nothing happened. It was like she was awake in a body that was sleeping. She *was* awake, but her body was asleep, and wouldn't wake up.

She panicked and the room around her started to bend in on itself. The walls and ceiling and floor tried to swallow her up in collapsing geometric unfoldment. Suddenly she remembered the words the man spoke: Your heart knows what's best for you and will never deceive you.

She listened to the beating in her chest. A nice calm steady rhythm, like it was unaware of the hell she perceived herself going through. 'Your dreams have been built on fear...', she heard echo in her head. She stopped thinking the room was trying to swallow her, and in an instant the walls and ceiling and floor retracted.

She listened to the beat of her own heart, in full awareness of it for the first time in her life. The room gradually glowed a golden orange, like a light from her heart was illuminating it. With every beat it grew brighter. She was no longer afraid.

She stepped up out of her body and looked back at it sleeping. For the first time in forever, the lurking sadness was not within her. She saw a door and walked through it.

She entered a bedroom where a man was asleep in a bed. It was the man from her dreams. She approached the bed and gently squeezed his hand. His eyes slowly peeled open, and he looked at her in shock.

You done it, he croaked.
I did, replied Scarlett.
Now let me get you out of here, the man said.

The man raised from bed fully dressed, like he was prepared for this moment all along. He picked her up. She wrapped her legs around his waist, her arms around his neck, and he carried her out of the room.

They were back in the house in which Scarlett was trapped.

The man navigated the house, from doorway to doorway. Room to room. Staircase to staircase. The house was like a maze, but the man seemed to know his way around it. It was decorated like it was from the time Scarlett's parents would have been her age.

Through the labyrinth of the house they travelled. The man found a laundry chute. Holding Scarlett tightly, he climbed into it. Sliding down, they emerged at a small flight of stairs, with the front door before them. The man straightened up, strengthening his grip on Scarlett he walked towards the door.

Stop, Scarlett shouted.

The man looked down into her eyes. She kissed him, hugging his neck tightly. It was the first time she had ever kissed anyone. The man's beard prickled her lips. She didn't care that he was old. She felt safe and loved in his arms.

A fire arose within her, dancing its way from between her legs into her heart.

Parting, their eyes met in silence.

The man gently pecked her on her cheek,

understanding what she was feeling.

I'm not here to do that, he laughed, scanning her face for rejection. But what you feel is love. And love gets you out of where fear has kept you trapped. What awaits you on the otherside of that door, is freedom from fear. What awaits you on the otherside of that door, is love. Love like you've never known before.

Scarlett smiled, her freckled face aglow with the light from her eyes.
I understand, she said, embracing the man tightly.

Now, let's get you home, the man said as he kicked the door open into blinding sunlight.

Scarlett gently awakened. Stretching her arms and legs, she yawned like a lion. Her eyes blinked open to see her real bedroom. She loved it so much. She felt the crisp white sheets of her bed on her skin. A cool breeze blew in through the window, as birds sang their morning song.

She sat up in bed and looked down at her legs. A small patch of bright red blood was on the sheets. She understood. She was unafraid of it. She knew she had become a woman.

Scarlett, she heard her mother call, your breakfast is ready.

Chain Breakers Inc.

Juliette The Liberator
Juliette The Liberator was the managing director of an agency called Chain Breakers Incorporated. Their slogan was: "You Don't Have To Have A Shackle On Your Ankle To Be A Slave".

She embodied The Goat of Mercury, with The Horse of Jupiter, along with a little Mermaid of The Moon, but her heart beat with the fire of Mars. She had pitch black hair, dyed bright orange.

She came from a mob of roaming Gypsies. The most notorious gang of The Old World. A band of outlaws, a family of robbing hoods.

When her mother, the head of the gang, passed, Juliette was bestowed with role of New Mother. Her first mission as New Mother was to liberate her sister from The Family.

This was a tough first mission, but her sister's work was done with The Family, as she was the one who guided their mother to death. She was The Plutonian Boatwoman who brought their mother Home.

With mother safely Home, The Family could now receive instructions from The Otherside. Their mother spoke to them through songs and books and movies, and told them everything they needed to know, to live comfortably in The New World.

Juliette was instructed to set up a business with a sleeping partner. This sleeping partner, she was told, would re-enter her life after leaving it for a while. She would remember him, and know that he was only here to do good. The recently liberated sister was the one who would bring them together again.

And so, today we find Juliette sat in her office, waking and baking and painting her toenails. Her feet atop the clear perspex desk she sat behind, her Red Bottoms kicked off into the middle of the floor.

Ishi-O
Ishi-O was her other sister, one of her employees, and former Master of Disguise when in the most notorious gang known to The Old World.

She embodied The Mantis of Uranus, with The Goat of Mercury, along with a little Horse of Jupiter. But her heart beat with the weirdness of Uranus. Her hair sat in a three-foot circumference from her head, the winner of Best Afro In The New World – 1979.

This morning we find her bringing coffee to Juliette in her office.

So, Juliette said taking a sip, what cases are you working on today?

Well, d'you remember the man from last week. The one who wanted me to go and see a house with him?

Hmmm, Juliette pondered, shaking her head.

Well, this man rang last week. He told me he needed help and asked if I would accompany him to a house. He gives me the address and I meet him there. The house was for sale, a mansion more than a house. The Big White House he called it.

Thinking of buying it, I asked him. He was. He had the keys and we went inside to have a look about. As we're going up the stairs he turns and says to me: I used to live here you know. Yeah I grew up here. This is my old bedroom, he signalled to the first room at the top of the stairs.

We go in and he starts telling all these stories from his childhood. He tells me he had a dream. A dream of me and him standing here in this room, having this very same conversation. It doesn't faze me, I've heard weirder. I say to him: So, do you think you'll take it? Yeah, he replies, I think I will. Just have to move some money about. I nod, then ask: So... why am I here?

He turns and looks at me dead in the eye: When I buy it, I want you to burn it down for me. OK, I nod, to make it look like arson? No, he answers, and here's the clinker, he says: I want you to fly a plane into it. I smile, thinking he's being sarcastic. His expression is unmoving. He just raises his eyebrows as if to say: Well?

I'm going to have to think about that, I tell him. May I ask why?

This house holds too many ghosts of the past. And the only way to rid them is with fire. Explosive bombastic fire.

So that was you that hijacked the plane at the weekend? Juliette asked.

Yeah, never a dull moment, Ishi-O laughed. So, she continued, what's The Boss up to? And will I ever get to meet him?

The person she referred to as The Boss was Chain Breakers Incorporated sleeping partner.

Juliette laughed: Maybe you already have. Last time we spoke he was engineering a virus.

What kind of virus? Asked Ishi-O.

A sort of super-flu. At least that's what he's planning to sell it to the government as. It's really no more harmful than a mild cold. But when you sell something as a super-flu, and the media start listing the symptoms, the first sign of the sniffles and average Joe convinces themself they've got it.

He told me, it's not the virus that will kill people, it's the fear of getting it. If they do get infected, their belief in the strength of their own immune system will either kill them or free them.

He's never done freeing people eh. So, Ishi-O pondered, if you don't believe it will kill you, it won't?

Exactly.

And, the idiots who believe everything they're told are the one's who'll die.

Exactly.

He has already infected himself with it, to become immune. He'll probably start running test trials soon, if you want me to put your name forward.

Sign me up, Ishi-O exclaimed. Any idea why he started it?

Fucking eBay buyers!

For real?

Yeah, some kind of revenge plot that he has been planning. Around the time I did that big job for him, he had sold everything he owned on eBay. But you know what eBay buyers are like.

Yeah, fucking wankers.

Yeah, the majority of people who bought his stuff ended up complaining, as they do, looking fucking partial refunds, claiming stuff was faulty. He said to me, the anonymity of the internet makes people think they're untouchable. They think that anonymity allows them to be rude, and you know

how he feels about rude people.
Yikes.

So, he has this list of addresses of everyone who fucked him over from eBay, while he was working on this virus. Why not combine them he thinks. So he designs a government pamphlet warning about a new super-flu in the area, infects the pamphlet with the virus, so once a person touches it, it's on their fingers, next time they touch their mouth, that's them infected.

When people are reading something that scares them, what's the first thing their body instinctively does?

They cover their mouth with their hand.

Bingo. He sent these to his list of eBay dickheads, sat back and waited for the news to come in. Slowly reports came. He ticked off each name from his list with the corresponding news report. That's when he knew it worked.

Ruthless. That's cause and affect I suppose. Someone's gotta play Shiva.

Someone's gotta do it, before the world is over-run by self-righteous money grabbing fuckers.

And idiots.

That's one big ass chain being broke. Does he have a name for the virus?
Yeah, answered Juliette, he's calling it The Flood.

The Bee Keeper

When Archie McBurney breathed in his body crackled in licking flames, from blue to gold to pink. When Archie McBurney breathed out, he expelled a fire ball 18 feet in diameter around his body.

He wasn't always like this; Once, he was a flicker that barely flamed. Now he lived in The Haus Of Fire, now he was The Haus Of Fire.

Ever since childhood Archie McBurney was plagued with nightmares. He would awake into the dark stillness of his bedroom, damp with cold sweat. Even as a teenager he was still a scared little boy when he descended into the realm of dream.

In the realm of dream you will be treated as you appear. So, Archie McBurney was treated like a scared little boy in the realm of dream.

One day Archie McBurney was minding his own business, kicking stones, while out walking in the countryside. The sun kissed his skin, the wind talked in gentle whirls, Earth solid and comforting beneath his feet. The sound of a nearby stream swirled and burped.

Archie McBurney bothered no one, hoping no one would bother him. But today, this was not to be.

As he surveyed the peaceful surroundings, his eye caught a group of boys up ahead. Three of them he counted, standing around a great birch tree. Panic rose in his stomach and he felt sick. He slowed his pace and thought about turning back. Just as the idea came to him to retreat, one of the boys looked up in his direction. I can't turn back now, Archie thought, I'll look like a coward.

He swallowed hard and continued walking, his eyes to his feet. From the periphery of his vision, he saw the boys taking notice of him. Silently signalling to each other with elbows in the ribs. I wish I was invisible, Archie wished, but didn't imagine.

As he grew closer to the three boys gathered around the great birch tree, he felt a sharp ding on his head. He closed his eyes tight to the pain, keeping his hands by his side, when all he wanted to do was raise them to the hurt. Then another sharp ding on his cheek, and the sound of a stone falling at his feet.

He reluctantly looked to the boys. One stood forward, a hand full of stones, the other hand poised to launch the offending artillery between thumb and forefinger. Archie watched as it sailed through the air, hitting him right on his upper lip as he tried unsuccessfully to swat it away.

He quickened his pace to get past them faster. Their collective laughs and jeers rising like a black hole the closer he got. His lip felt warm. He brought his tongue to it, tasted blood, and felt like crying.

Hey dickhead, came the words as he came level with the great birch tree. He ignored them, feeling the presence of hatred emanating from the boys around the birch. As he cast his eyes to his feet again, he felt a hefty thump on his back. It knocked the wind out of him, he fell to his knees gasping.

Hey dickhead, I'm talking to you: Were the words he heard, woven through the beating of his heart in his ears. He looked to the boy who had assumed command of the uprising, and not knowing how to reply, he let out a nervous laugh.

Are you fucking laughing at me? Were the next words he heard, said with more anger than mocking. Archie laughed again. Stop fucking laughing at me, came the reply.

Archie rose to his feet and prepared his legs for a sprint. As if the boys had realised this, another sprung at him and caught him in a headlock. He pulled and dragged him in circles. Archie's feet wind-milling through dust and gravel.

Archie's face reddened as the headlock tightened around his throat. He coughed and choked as strings of spittle dangled from his mouth. He had never felt so embarrassed in his life, so much so, that he started to cry.

The boy dumped him on the ground, as the other two gathered around. They seemed colossal, their shadows closing in on him. As they laughed, all Archie could think was: Please leave me alone now.

He waited for the sound of retreating footsteps, his head buried under his arms, but they never came. The laughing had stopped, but their stares cut into him like lasers.

He slowly pulled himself up. Dusting the dirt from his trousers he found them ripped at the knees, bloody skin peeking from underneath. He rose to the silent grinning faces of the three boys around him in a circle. He avoided any eye contact, and turning sidewards, slipped out of the circle, pushing past their unmoving shoulders.

A dozen footsteps ahead and another stone ricocheted from the back of his neck, where the spine meets the skull. He winched with clenched shoulders as the words: Fucking faggot, echoed behind him.

Archie felt empty inside as the sunlight caused his swollen eye to shut even more. He rubbed his ribs and head and padded his lip with his thumb. Adrenaline billowed through his torso to the point he couldn't catch his breath. He wanted to stop, bend over, hold his knees and take a series of deep breaths, but he could still feel the presence of the boys around the birch, and decided to keep walking, hoping beyond hope that he didn't pass out.

But pass out he did. Thankfully, for his self-esteem, this occurred out of eyeshot of his attackers. The world turned inside out in front of his eyes, and the last thing he remembered was stumbling to the grass, lest his head become a pin cushion for gravel, dirt and stones.

Then darkness.
Then quietness.
Then stillness.

Then nothing.

Archie slowly regained consciousness to a low vibrational hum. The hum fluctuated in droning waves of thick sound, unending and with an undercurrent of immense menace. For a brief moment, he forgot everything, and felt like he always wanted to, like he didn't exist. Then his memory broke through the dam of nothingness, and he felt like vomiting. The pain returned. His knees, ribs, head, eye and lip pulsed in perfectly timed rhythmic synchronisation. It was like his body was singing a painful hymn of agony.

And what was that humming drone in his ears?

Ah, you're awake, came a soft voice from above and behind. Here, drink this.

Archie McBurney opened his eye that would open and looked at the blurred image of a polystyrene cup of water being held to his lips. He sipped through his swollen mouth, the cool water, a tang of blood. Hoisting himself into his elbow, he saw he had been lying on a wooden bench, with a thick jacket around him.

The vibrational buzz grew louder as he brought

himself up.

Thank you, he said to the disembodied voice.

I found you lying at the back of my field, I saw what happened, the voice said, them boys picking on you and all. I was going to intervene, but something stopped me. As I watched, I just felt it was something you had to go through.

Archie McBurney didn't know if he should feel grateful or offended. He sat up, with his head in his hands. The disembodied voice sat beside him, the weight creaking the bench.

Archie McBurney turned to look at the voice for the first time. He recoiled in a slight gasp at the sight of a smiling face beneath a wide brimmed white hat, underneath a white netted veil.

A thick padded white arm reached out, revealing a fat white glove through the sleeve, that looked like it was made of marshmallows.

Pleased to meet you, the face behind the veil said, I'm The Bee Keeper.

Ah, Archie internally realised.

My name's Archie, he said giving the marshmallow hand an awkward shake.

Bit of a tizz you got yourself into earlier, The Bee Keeper said, how do you feel?

How long was I out for? Archie asked without answering.

Not long, about half an hour. I watched the whole thing. You walking past; them starting on you; you stumbling off and fainting into the grass. Like I said, I would have helped but there are just some things we have to go through in life. You've got to learn how to stand up for yourself boy.

I'm a pacifist, Archie said.

Me too, replied The Bee Keeper. But has being a pacifist ever stopped you from getting bullied before? Or are you using that word as a shield from conflict?

Archie shrugged his shoulders, half understanding what was being said to him.

The Bee Keeper patted him on the back.

I was the same as you...Archie, is it? Archie nodded.
I was picked on, bullied, beat up, easily led, led astray and taken advantage of. Until I became The Bee Keeper. Bees were the one thing I was never afraid of. Never stung, never have been. I was terrified of everything else. That world, those people. But when I started working with the bees, I realized that all the bullies in the world, were the most terrified of all. They get on how they do, because they are terrified that one-day they will come across someone who gets on in a way that scares them. And they can't handle fear. Just the

same as their fathers couldn't handle fear. Do you see what I'm saying? The ones who are most afraid of life will portray themselves not to be.

The bees told me that, The Bee Keeper said topping up Archie's water from a large plastic container, then taking a swig for himself.

He continued, waving a marshmallow finger in the air: The sound of a swarm of bees: if you really listen to it you will realise how they speak. Then, when you understand their language, you can talk to them.

The Bee Keeper read Archie McBurney's slight look of worry, so he extrapolated:
I know it sounds crazy. But there is far more to this world than you've ever been told. Most of it is invisible. You must learn how to live in the invisible aspect of the world, as well as the visible aspect of .
it. The invisible aspect of the world becomes visible when we fall asleep. When we dream.
How are your dreams Archie?

Full of nightmares, he answered.

Of course they are. Mine were too. But when I became The Bee Keeper, all I could think about was bees. I was around them so much, that even when I wasn't, I felt like I was. The last thing I would think about before falling asleep, was having all my bees around me.

You see? You must learn to see yourself as more than you are. It is your imagined version of yourself who will slay the monsters of your nightmares, not this scared little boy sitting beside me all beaten and bruised.

I'm not sure I understand, said Archie.

Well, the dream world, the invisible world, is powered by imagination. Put simply: if you imagine yourself to be a doormat, you will get walked upon. If you imagine yourself to be surrounded by bees, no one, or nothing, will come near you in fear of being stung.
Belief and imagination are the key to it all. And both are limited only by one's own fear of their own power. The power of the fist is nothing compared to the power of the mind.

Watch this.

The Bee Keeper rose and pulled off his veiled hat. He kicked off his boots, unzipped his padded suit, stepped out of it and pulled his gloves off with his teeth.

Here he stood in front of Archie McBurney in a faded blue denim shirt, brown denim jeans with green socks on his feet. He extended his hand again, to be shook without glove. This time Archie McBurney could feel his skin, could see the person under that suit.

Buzz Beesly, The Bee Keeper said introducing himself. But everyone just calls me The Bee Keeper. Our names hold the clues to what we are meant to become.

Now, he said raising a finger, if you believe something enough you can do anything.

With that The Bee Keeper walked towards the hives of bees. With each step he undid a button of his shirt, slipping out of the arms, he let it fall.

He undid his jeans and left them where he stepped out of them. Pulling a sock off each foot, he lastly pulled down his boxer shorts, and kicked them to the side.

The Bee Keeper turned to Archie McBurney, in all his nakedness. Flesh, pubes and penis.

Imagination Archie, he shouted from the gateway to the hives: Imagination is the key to never being fucked with again.

With that he turned, unlatched the gate and walked naked into the swarming mass of beehives.

Archie closed his eyes and imagined himself on fire. Then imagined a ball of fire surrounding his body.

When he opened them, he saw The Bee Keeper slowly waving to him. Smiling from a cocoon of a million bees around his body.

The Quiet Man

The Quiet Man was a loud boy. One day he was disciplined for being noisy and locked in The Tower of Soundlessness.

Here, for nine years he perfected: The power to kill with silence.

The Quiet Man was an Eawning Master. He could slow time to the point he could catch bullets in the quietude of the moment.

He invented the following techniques to help others achieve Illumination while imprisoned in The Tower of Soundlessness:

The Cold Water Rebirth.
A technique where The Worker is submerged in cold water and performs Billowing Infinity.

The Sleeping River.
A technique where The Worker heals another by syncopating their breaths, connected by the stomach and chest.

Breathing the Body Electric.
A technique where the Worker expands their energetic field from the heart, moving left to right, up and down and forwards and backwards in one movement.

Billowing Infinity.

A technique where The Worker breathes like a circle, while moving their legs in a billowing rhythm, in time with the breath.

The Contraction and Expansion Of Pain.
A technique where The Worker focuses on pain in the body. With the imagination they shrink the pain inwards while expanding the body outwards.

The Vertical Waveform.
A technique where The Worker pushes the heart upwards and the naval backwards in a constant motion.

Seated Lighthouse.
A technique where The Worker holds their shoulders and turns the torso right to left in a constant motion. Allowing the energy of the heart to emanate from the movement of the arms.

Cliffhanger.
A technique where The Worker lifts and drops their shoulders to and from their ears.

Dance of The Divine Pulse.
A technique where The Worker contracts the perineum upward to release energy into the body, then relaxes it down to fill the auric field.

While locked in The Tower of Soundlessness for 9 years, The Quiet Man underwent The Reconfiguration of The Five Senses. He lost his hearing, sight, smell, taste and ability to feel. When these finally returned they were twice as strong as before.

During the last year of his imprisonment he performed The Procedure Of Saints on himself. Which is a self-vasectomy, for The Quiet Man was not to be a father of children, but a father of ideas.

The Portal Opener

The Portal Opener was sat beside a hospital bed, in conversation with a dying woman.

'Once you leave here, you're going to want to send messages back. Once you leave here, you will see what's really going on. You're going to be sorry about your actions and words against those that were only doing good. With every insult you've ever thrown at me, I've turned the other cheek, because I know what is going on here. And once you see all this shit from the other side, you're going to realise that the people you hurt with your words and your actions, were the open portals for you to communicate with this world. I am that open portal, for I am The Portal Opener. Your words and actions, especially against the open portals leave a residue that you have to clean up. And that's a whole lot of hell once you experience life on the other side. As The Portal Opener I can help clean that residue up for you. And do you know all you have to do for that help to be accepted: Watch your tongue. In these last moments of your life, think very seriously about that, for the train is coming to pick you up shortly. Here is something to remember if you need to return here: The trick of life is to die many times before the body dies. With each living death you move up a level. If you just wait to die when the body is used up, you only go up one level. A level you could have achieved while still living. Never forget, and you will see very shortly, that life is a game, the greatest game you could ever play. So next time, if there is one, learn to play the game of life. Now, you may die.'

The Portal Opener rose from his seat, picked up his overcoat and draped it over his right arm. He walked out of the room, gently closing the door behind him. Nodding to the nurses on duty, he made his way to the elevator. Just as he pressed the arrow pointing down, he noticed the nurses rushing to the room he had just left.

He smiled, closed his eyes, took a deep breath, and let the ding of the elevator fill his ears. Opening his eyes, he stepped in and pressed 0. You won't believe the things I've seen, said an invisible voice in his head. Believe me, I have, he thought-spoke, have fun. And give me a shout sometime when our back's need scratched.

The Switch Hitter

To switch someone off, you pressed the solar plexus area with the second and third fingers of your left hand, while pressing the nape of the neck, with the thumb of your right hand.

This was best done from behind. Then they'd never know what hit them.

There are three levels to switching someone off. A quick press and they will trance out. Hold it for one second and they will lose consciousness. Hold it for three seconds and they will die.

You used these at your discretion, depending on the job.

The training to be a Switch Hitter lasted nine years. In that time, you would disappear from your old life and be given a new identity, a new character to play.

Payment for any job was never done with money. Switch Hitters didn't have bank accounts. They got paid in things.

If you did a job for a property-developer, you'd be paid with property. For a car dealer, you'd get an automobile. A butcher, a years supply of meat. A hooker, the worlds greatest blowjob. Their social status depended on your payment.

The Switch Hitter wasn't concerned with how big or small the payment was. Only that it was truly in balance with the person paying. A hooker would never be expected to pay with real estate. A property developer would never be expected to pay with the worlds greatest blowjob.

Switch Hitters were peaceful people. That's why they chose that job. With it came solitude.

In the nine years of training they were taught how to develop their intuition to the point they were telepathic. No one ever contacted them about a job. A Switch Hitter would know when to place themselves in the right scenario, around the right people who needed a job done, without a word being spoke.

When not working, Switch Hitters usually practised Eawning, to place them in a meditative state: Cooking, cleaning, gardening, painting, playing an instrument. Something you could do and didn't have to think about, an action of pure intuition.

In that state you are open to The Invisible World. In that state you can communicate with The Others in The Invisible World. If a job needed doing, it was here you'd receive the time and location. Sometimes it would flash in the mind's eye, like a photograph being taken. Sometimes it was felt emotionally.

During The Outbreak, parks were best to pick up work. After The Outbreak, bars were best. Somewhere you could sit and not be noticed.

After a couple of drinks people loosen up and start to talk about all the shit they're afraid to mention when sober: How much they hated their husband. How their business partner fucked them over. How this creep felt them up when they were drunk.

A Switch Hitter's ears were always open. During training they learn how to listen to silence. Once you've mastered listening to silence, listening to someone's conversation at the other end of a noisy bar is nothing.

Switch Hitters never carried money. If they needed it, they would walk up behind someone, switch them off with a quick press, dip into their pocket, and be on their way. When the person came to, after a few seconds, they would think they had just had a dizzy spell. And when they realised their bank card was missing, they thought they must have left it at the last shop they used it.

Again: bars are the best place to do this.

So you'd be sitting in the corner of a bar, ears scanning the room, hearing all types of shit. But what you were listening for is a certain way people speak. To be exact, you would listen for the sound of vengeance being sought.

Even if they were drinking alone, you could tell it in how they ordered a drink. Once you heard that tone, you'd silence every other noise and zone-in on that one person or conversation.

Once you got the crux of it, you'd wait for that right

time to make your presence known: Can I get you a drink? Where do I know your face from? The classics never failed.

A Switch Hitter is a master of disguise. They at once look nondescript and like no one else around them, like an old Hell's Angel in a country pub, or an old man at a rave.

The Mystery School

The Rainbow Crook
The Man arrives at The Mystery School. All his belongings are burned. He is washed and his body shaved. He is shown where to sleep, eat and defecate. He is escorted to a darkened room, lit by a lone candle. The Teacher sits. The Teacher beckons The Man to sit.
The Man sits.

The Man is told to press his tongue to the roof of his mouth, while pulsing his perineum rhythmically, in time to his heart.

Inhaling through his nose, he imagines a rainbow rising up his spine, round his head, past his nose, to the roof of his mouth. Making the shape of a crook.
The Rainbow Crook.

Without pausing before the next breath, he exhales through the nose. Imagining the rainbow moving past his chin, neck, chest, stomach back to his perineum.

Without pausing before the next breath, he inhales the rainbow up the spine, round to the roof of the mouth, exhaling down the front.

The Man is told that keeping the tongue pressed to the roof of the mouth, gives the rainbow a bridge to move from the heart to the head.

He is told the exclusion of gaps in the breath creates a unifying flow.

The Man does this six times at his natural breathing speed, on the seventh he slows the pulsing of his perineum down to half the speed of his heart.

He inhales slowly and deeply, allowing the rainbow to rise to his heart.
He retains his breath for six beats of his heart, on the seventh he inhales gently allowing the rainbow to pass from the heart to the brain.
He feels it expand in his head, and slowly exhales.

The Man removes his tongue from the roof of his mouth, returning his breathing to normal. He listens to the beating of his heart with full body awareness.

He stays like this for the next two hours, once a day for the next seven years.

The Three Boxes
The Man is brought to The Quiet Room. It is completely square, around 15 feet on each side, walls black and soft.
A pillow in the centre. The Man sits.

The Whispering Voice instructs The Man to imagine his body glowing, like every pore is reaching out to hear the silence of The Quiet Room.
The Man listens with his pores.

The Whispering Voice instructs The Man in the construction of mental imagery in the creative

imagination. The Man creates The Three Boxes.
The box in the middle represents The Now, to the
left The Was, to the right The What.

When The Man is in The Quiet Room, any thoughts
that interrupt, are put into one of these boxes.

The Man does this for an hour each day for the
next seven years.

Over time The Man starts to remember everything
that has ever happened to him since he arrived in
the womb of his mother.

The Rod and The Ring
The Man is shown an image of a rod placed on
top of a ring. It is here he places his ego. For it is
against the ego's nature to be seen to fall, so it
balances.

The Placenta
The Man goes to The Quiet Room.
He imagines his body glowing, every pore listening
to The Quiet.
He speaks words to evoke The Placenta, in hope of
conversation.
He does this 20 minutes a day, for three months.

One day The Placenta speaks.
He shows The Man the map back Home.
The Man starts to walk it.
One day The Placenta speaks his name.
One day The Man knows his name.

The Star Of David
The Man is brought to a room of pale wooden
floors and white walls. Light fills the space without
windows.

He sits on a chair in the centre of the room.
The Whispering Voice comes through, telling him
of The Star Of David. The Star Of David is the
shape of his Light Body, in which his Heavy Body
exists. It is two triangles on top of each other, one
facing up, one facing down. The Man imagines this
shape three dimensionally, with himself in the
middle.

The peak of each triangle, over his head, below his
feet, are in alignment with The Man's spine.

The Man sees the triangle pointing down, rotating
to his right. This is his connection to Earth/Mother.
The Man sees the triangle pointing up, rotating to
his left. This is his connection to The Sun/Father.

The Man imagines a blazing sun shining in his
belly, it's centre at his navel. It expands to fill the
entire stomach area, up to the solar plexus, down
to the perineum.

The Man inhales through his nose into this sun,
pushing his belly out. He sees it glow brighter. The
Man retains his breath and watches it blaze.
The Man purses his lips and blows out the mouth,
seeing the sun expanding from his belly,
surrounding his body in all directions.

He inhales through the nose, imagining the sun moving from his belly to his heart. He retains his breath and imagines his heart and chest area glowing with a golden green light.
He purses his lips and blows out his mouth, imagining the golden green light expanding from his heart to surround his body.

The Man takes a deep inhalation, breathing right down to his perineum. He imagines The Divine Spark of pure golden white light there. He retains his breath. The Man sees the counter rotating triangles of The Star Of David spinning at the speed of light.

As this movement stabilises, The Divine Spark shines brighter and brighter. The Man takes a short inhalation, pursing his lips, he blows out of his mouth seeing the golden white light expanding from his perineum, to surround the body. It moves out in a disk shape, creating a field of golden white light to a radius of 18 feet around his body.

The Man inhales. He sees The Divine Spark creating The Torsion Field. It is the shape of a hollowed-out apple, running from his perineum to his heart, and out the top of his head.

The Man senses The Torsion Field in constant flow, as his breath returns to its resting rhythm.

The Man stays in Unity Consciousness for the rest of the day. He does this each day for the next year.

The Aria Of Trinity
The Man has a stable Star of David. One day he is brought to the room with pale wooden floors and white walls, filled with windowless light. The Whispering Voice tells him it is now time to align The Song Of The Heart with The Aria Of Trinity.

The Man sits.

The Man brings his awareness to his heart and asks for its song. It sings in his ears. He listens to the song with his entire body, like every cell is reaching out to hear it.

He sees Earth below his feet. He travels to its heart where The Mother resides. He offers his love back to Her. The Mother senses The Man's love is not pure enough yet. The Man returns each day and offers his love back for the next six months.

One day The Mother accepts The Man's love back. She sings The Song Of The Heart as it expands in The Man's ears.

He travels from the heart of Earth, through his heart, and out the top of his head. He sees The Sun above him. He travels to its heart and asks The Father to receive his love back into his heart. The Father senses The Man's love is not pure enough yet. So he returns once a day for the next six months until it is.

One day The Father accepts The Man's love back. He sings the Song Of The Heart as it expands in The Man's ears.

The Man achieves The Aria Of Trinity, as three hearts sing as one. He travels back to his heart where he sits in song for the rest of the week.

Sitting At The Knee Of The Dark Goddess
The Man is Sitting At The Knee Of The Dark Goddess. He confronts the darkness in hope of understanding it. He thinks about everything he was told not to. He looks where he never looked. He understands trauma and pain and hurt and anger and jealousy and all the things he tried to forget. He gives attention to the unhealed and it heals.

The Whispering Voice speaks: Everything happens to us for a reason. That reason is to awaken us. You must remember Truth. The traumas trigger awakenings of Truth.

Jailbreaking Reality
The Man is given The Holy Plant to ingest. The Holy Plant thins the veil between worlds. The Man lives in two worlds at once.

The Man is given The Sacred Fungi to ingest. The Man encounters beings who have realised their full creative potential and look like nothing he has seen before. They show The Man how to realise his full creative potential, so he can look like nothing they have seen before.

The Thing They Told You Not To Do
One early morning The Man is taken to a bench on top of a hill. He sits and watches The Sun rise, holding his gaze on it as long as he can. He does

this each morning for an hour, understanding the quality of each season through its light, for the next year.

One day, The Sun speaks to The Man.

The Game Designer

The Game Designer designed a virtual reality multiplayer game, where The Player picked a world and storyline, then inserted themselves into it as the main character and their friends as the co-stars. Because what is a story without friends.

He had constructed The Sleep Pod. This is where the game took place after The Player had picked the world, storyline and character they wanted to play.

The Sleep Pod was a large orb The Player stood inside. It was in here they would play The Game until finished.

Once in The Sleep Pod, The Game was fed into the orb with invisible vapour. When inhaled The Player fell into a conscious trance and The Game was projected onto the holographic lining of The Sleep Pod, immersing The Player in their game of choosing.

The Game Designer had found a way to translate computer coding into invisible vapour, which he called: Gyxeon.

Gyxeon acted as an amnesiac sedative, and lasted until The Game was over, making The Player forget they were even playing a game in the first place. And that was the main reason behind The Game: To remember it was a game while playing it.

To make things easier, The Game Designer inserted certain consumable substances within The Game. These eased the Gyxeon during game play, allowing The Player to have insightful experiences that helped them remember they were playing a game, while in The Game.

While designing their game, The Player chose a type of family they wanted to be born into and experience The Game with. A few of the choice titles were:
The Neurotic Mother. The Single Mother. The Alcoholic Father. The Single Father. Sibling Rivalry. The Only Child. The Step-Child. The Middle Child. To name but a few.

These family experiences could be configured whatever way The Player wished to experience them. With the simulation of childbirth began The Players entry into The Game.

The whole point of The Game was to remember it was a game, while playing The Game. The majority of players died before being reawakened in The Sleep Pod and only then, remembering they were playing a game.

When this happened, most wanted to play again. It was that good. People couldn't stop going back for more.

An integral part of the experience were the clues planted throughout it. The Player would pick certain objects, moments and people that would appear during it that blatantly reminded them they were playing a game. But the opposition in The Game would try to convince them otherwise.

The opposition was a key part of The Game. It was in the media they consumed, it was played by family and friends, and most of all it was played by the assumed leaders of the world of The Game: A shadowy elite of highly perverted megalomaniacs. Their greed for power was matched only by the desperate frustration they felt as it constantly wriggled out of their grasping, grabbing hands.

It was up to The Player to figure out that this world, this game they were playing was of their own creation. They allotted a time-frame to do this in, usually between 60-80 game years. If they didn't work it out by then, The Game ended. A simulation of death was experienced, constructed by their life choices, and they awoke back in The Sleep Pod.

If they did work it out, the world opened up as a free roaming game, everything was unlocked, and they got to enjoy the experience of their own making until they were ready to not play any longer.

This was the winning of The Game. Most who made it to this level decided to stay on and help others who were trapped in their version of The Game. Some expert players played over and over again, just to help other players who were stuck on certain levels.

The Player chose a setting, a moment in time, a stage on which to play their game. These were picked from a list of choices. Only upon winning The Game, did they get to design their own level. Some of these choices were:

The Utopian Future Level. The World War II Level. The Egyptian Level. The Jesus Level. The Rock Star Level. The Starving African Family Level. The War-torn Country Level. The Dystopian Future Level. The Medieval Level. The First-Person Alive Level. The Millionaire Level. The Monk Level. The Last Person Alive Level. The Royal Family Level.

There were twelve characters The Player could choose to play The Game as. Only upon winning did they get to design their own character. The choices were:

The Innovator. The Infiltrator. The Twins. The Empath. The Leader. The Advisor. The Diplomat. The Mystic. The Adventurer. The CEO. The Outcast. The Psychic.

Within The Game there were ten levels to be completed before winning. At the end of each, The Player went up against The End Of Level Bosses. When overcome The Player would then gain the attributes of each boss. The ten End Of Level Bosses were:

The Healer. The Warrior. The Boss. The General. The Lover. The King. The Magician. The Creative. The Guide. The Companion.

When The Player had taken on all the attributes from these Bosses they had won The Game and now were known as The Hero.

At this point they were now free to create their own world and characters within it. They got to enjoy their own creations for as long as they wished, then they pressed Exit Game.

The Namer Of Things

And so, one day The Man as a child wrote a list of art he would one day make, as soon as the tech matched the vision.
Once you know the name, then you can create.

BOOK ONE
First You Will Learn From The Ancestors Of Earth. How To Integrate Your Hidden Energy. New Language Is Born. The Integration Begins. And Let Chaos Reign Supreme. Welcome To The Lodge Of All Knowledge. Remember The Beauty In Your Own Truth. How Simple it All Really Is. The Guides Emerge. The Man Emerges. Within Nature Are The Codes Of Life. Your Brain When The Realisation Hits. The Growth Of Knowledge Comes From All. The Power You Hold Is Revealed. Re-Emerge Yourself With The Forest. The Three Yours. In Dreams Knowledge Is Told. One Day He Will Visit. So Don The Robes Of Your Truth. Welcome To The Light.

Songs Of The Abyss
A Bridge Between Worlds. A Portal Awaits Re-Entry. And One Day It All Came Crashing Down. Hark An Angel Sing. Ascension Seen From The Top. Old Fences Now Open. Old Tools Of Slavery. Reach Up And Touch The Light. Seven Steps Of The Sun. Pluto From Planet Mondo. The Darkness Awaits. Sounding The Call. The Naked Mother. Thrones Of The Ancestors. They Came With A Message.

El-Lah. Miamerecha. Miamereel. Miamerees.
Miamerelu. Miameremu. Miamerepah.
Miamererah. Nayvayah

Expansion Of The Soul In Gold And Pink. Flight Of
The Eagle In Four Dimensions. Flight Of The
Shaman. In The Bosom Of The Great Mother.
Mask Of The Earth Mother. Reflections Of You.
Scales Of The Rainbow Serpent. The Downward
Motion Of The Golden Ascension Light. The
Elemental Kingdom In Colour. The Flight Path To
Matrix Liberation. The Upward And Downward
Expression Of Divine Love. The Upward Motion Of
Ascension. Unfolding Of The Axis. Birth Of The
Rainbow Serpent. Ceremonial Dancing Mask.
Chaos Magic In Pastels. Cross Section Of A 3rd
Dimensional Reality. Grounding Pattern Of Feet In
Nature. Hands Up Yeti. It Came From Lyra. Nine
Lives Down Nine To Go. Pixilated Nature Under A
Microscope. Kill the Bull for the Sacrifice. Shaman's
Head Dress. The Creative Power Of Love In Gold.
The Realisation That This Is It.

BOOK TWO
And It Was All So Simple. The World Was Not As
You Knew It. The Fires Of Awakening. The
Integration Progresses. The Crushing Resistance Of
Showing Your Full Potential. The Old World Slowly
Falls Away. Integration Of The Male. Balancing Of
The Male. A New Way To Communicate Is Born.
Then You Will Meet The Mother. Die Into Her Love.
Reborn As The Most Advanced Technology On This
Planet. Don't Be Afraid To Look At Your Darkness.
Procession Of The Fish God. The Three Ordeals

Towards The Sun/Son. Your Thoughts Are
Projecting Your Reality.

The Future Is Death
Crown Of Rebekkah. Mother Earth. The Heron.
The Light.

Jupiter. Mars. Mercury. Moon. Saturn. Sun. Venus.

Ascension To Jupiter. Castle Of Miamereel.
Collection Of Monuments. In The Belly Of The
Frog. Return To Mother Level Complete. Temple Of
Pan. Purse Of Hermes. Urn Of Ancestors.

BOOK THREE
The Union (Of The Three). They Told You You
Were Nothing (But You Are More Than Human).
Your Dreams Use Symbols To Talk To You (The
Dalmatians Dance The Shadow To Death). The
Hidden Hand Of Light Hides In Plain Sight (But You
Only See It When You Believe It). Inside Your Heart
There's A Room And Inside The Room Is A Box
(And Inside That Box Is Your Mission In Life). We
Are Individual Expressions Of The One (And Also
The One). Remove The Gaps In Your Breath And
See God (Or Hold It And Be It). All The Lives
You've Ever Lived Are Above Your Head (And You
Just Have To Look To See Them). Giant's Ring Is A
Light Body Activation Point (Once You Know What
That Is Go There). I Am The Light Given Off By The
Light (And Perfecting Myself Life After Life). We Are
The Creators Experiencing The Created (So Create
And Be Created). When You See This Place In Real
Life (Go To It And Tell Them You Saw It In A
Painting). Tell Someone Something Enough (And

They Believe It). Water Fire Air Earth (Mountain Of Grave Stones).

Nayvayah
In The Field Of Death Life Grows. Let The Beauty Of Your Suffering Show. Life Evolves From These Shapes. Life Is So Simple If You Let It Be. On The Vines Of Deliverance. Vase Of The Abyss. You Don't Fit In Because You're Not Meant To. Your Life Is Shit So You Might As Well Kill Yourself. Your Truth Will Set You Free.

Chapel Of The Temple. Gardens Grounds And 1st Floor. Gradients Of Man. Map Of The Female. Pulse Points In the Temple Of Man. Temple Of The Man. The Continuous Contraction And Retraction Of Life. The Haus As Star Of David. The Spheres Of Understanding.

Damien As The Moon. Eeon As the Sun. El Jaye As Mercury. Eli As Jupiter. Little Voice As Mars. Mondo As Pluto. Rebekkah As Venus. Sebastian As Earth. The Man As Saturn.

Ilsa

Germany – World War II
'We want that information', The Nazi Minister Of Occult Operations said, banging his desk with a leather gloved hand.

The Two Jews stayed silent.

'You tell us what you know, or we will extract it from you, using the most excruciating means possible.'

The Two Jews said not a word. Their gaze never once falling from the eyes of The Nazi Minister Of Occult Operations.

'If you do not divulge the secrets you keep from us, your defiance will only bring you suffering'

The Two Jews stayed defiant. Their wrists ached from the cords tying them behind their backs. Their knees pulsed and strained with pressure as they knelt on the cold concrete floor.

The Nazi Minister Of Occult Operations signalled to the two guards behind them. A rifle butt thudded each of their skulls and The Two Jews collapsed forward in a heap.

*

They awoke on a dirt floor, shackled in a windowless cell.

Each morning a group of guards, two male and one female, would enter and ask them if they were ready to divulge the information. And each morning, they refused. For their disobedience they were starved until they became skeletal.

One night The Female Guard came to their cell alone and spoke to them through the bars: You must tell them what they want to know. The Minister has drawn up a list of tortures he wants to subject you too until you speak. They will boil you in water. Freeze you in ice. Remove your finger nails. Insert objects inside of you. Flay your skin. Electrocute you. You must tell them what they want to know.

The Two Jews listened then turned their backs without saying a word.

She continued: To be honest with you, I didn't know what I was getting myself into when I joined up. I just got swept up in the hysteria of it all, and it has turned into an uncontrollable monster. I cannot bear to watch this suffering any longer. It is not who I am. I am a good woman, not a monster. Please just tell them what you know.

The Two Jews turned back to The Female Guard and approached the bars where she stood. For the first time one of them spoke:

If you want to help us… he looked to his friend, who finished the sentence for him…Then kill us.

*

For the next three months The Two Jews were tortured beyond belief. They were made to sit in boiling water until their blistering skin made them pass out from pain. Their feet were frozen in ice until their toes turned black. Each finger and toenail were pulled out with pilers. They had spiked metal objects inserted into their rectums until they fainted from blood loss. The skin was pealed from the palms of their hands and soles of their feet. They had their teeth pulled out. They had tremendous volts of electricity pass through their skulls until their bodies convulsed, their bowels emptying and eyes bleeding.

But they did not talk.

One night The Female Guard came to their cell alone again. The two people she saw no longer looked human. Black with blood and shit, bearded with long straggling hair. They were so thin they looked inside out.

She unlocked the cell and entered. The stench of blood, shit and bile was overwhelming. The Two Jews sat on the floor with their legs crossed, their eyes closed, in deep stillness. They looked like two emaciated Buddhas. Two arrow-struck Krishnas. Two crucified Christs.

The Female Guard unclipped her pistol from its holster and cocked the hammer. At this sound, The Two Jews opened their eyes. They looked at her and within their eyes swam only Truth. A light shone in blazing blue. The heave of tears rose from her chest into her throat, as she pointed the pistol to the head of the one closest to her, she traced her fingers over the handle of the gun, feeling the metalwork of the engraved swastika below them.

The Two Jews smiled at her and spoke in unison: Thank you. Until we meet again.

She shot them in succession, their bodies collapsing in bony heaps. They had died with the secrets they held, and for this The Minister would not be happy.

The Female Guard raised the pistol to her temple and blew her brains out, all over the cell wall. Her body collapsing on top of The Two Jews who she had helped retain secret knowledge that would one day change the world.

The Afterlife
After leaving their bodies The Two Jews and The Female Guard journeyed back through The Spheres Of Understanding, meeting The End Of Level Boss of each, and being shown their scoreboard. In that life these were known as The Planets.

They then arrived on Nayvayah, reunited with their Hauziz, and were shown the story of the lives they had just lived, which they watched like a virtual reality movie in front of their eyes.

On Nayvayah time does not exist. So, the three of them were free to explore this realm until they were ready for another game.

The Two Jews were rewarded for keeping safe the secret information from the Nazis. Their prize was that any lives they played from this point, they would do so as Masters.

Masters in disguise.

Masters in disguise as ordinary men. They were given the gift of being awake in a world asleep. All they had to do was leave information, hidden in literature, art and music, to help others awaken in a world asleep. Everything they needed to do this, was granted to them and they would struggle no longer.

The Female Guard was rewarded for helping The Two Jews, with the ability to also awaken in her next life. But that awakening would be worked for.

Before playing again the three devised an intertwining story where their paths would meet in their next game. Each meeting bringing an opportunity for Truth to be shown.

They picked what character they would play, which was represented by what star sign they were born under. Then shown the possibilities of what they could achieve if they understood those characters while alive.

The catch was that once they started The Game, they would forget all this. So, while designing their individual life stories, they placed certain things that would help them remember what they were there to do. Hidden messages within the art, literature and music of the world.

Once they had all this mapped out, the program for each player was inserted into their individual Sleep Pods, where they would experience the simulation of life.

And so, each entered their own Sleep Pod.

After they were sealed, the vapour blew in, the program started, and the experience commenced.

In a blaze of light, all three emerged into the wombs of their respective mothers, in a forming body which held the perfect parental personalities for the characters they had chosen to experience the world through.

And so, at different moments in the late 20th century, they entered what is known as Reality.

New York – 1979
One barman wore The Star Of David around his neck, one wore The Egyptian Ankh. They swung from gold chains, nestled in chest hair protruding from unbuttoned shirt collars.

The voices from the speakers sung the letters Y.M.C.A., and the heaving dance floor joined in. The Barmen pulled pints, and poured shots, and moved around each other with unspoken coordination, as a mass of voices shouted orders to them.

Booze, nicotine and cocaine filled the atmosphere. Disco was dying, but they were alive.

As the sun rose, and the birds sang, the bar emptied. The Barmen cashed up and swept the floor with ringing ears.

The door knocked, three times.

We're closed, they shouted in unison.

Silence.

Then a treble fistful of knocks again.

The Barmen looked at each other. One spoke: One more round of three makes nine...

Yeah, the other replied.

Silence.

Knock! Knock! Knock! Came the rhythmic beat of the door.

The Barmen looked to the Nazi dagger which hung above the bar they owned, the most famous gay biker bar on the lower east-side: The Shunt Roy.

They looked at each other and spoke at the same time:

It's her.

The Conversation

World War II was really a robbery of ancient knowledge. We have two bodies, made for two worlds. A heavy body for Earth, and a light body for Heaven. We can move between these bodies and worlds whenever we like.

Heaven is what people describe when they speak of The Future, so The Future is death, but you don't have to die to get there. It was from The Future that World War II was planned.

World War III is the final battle, it always was, the battle within. You enlist in it once you die while still alive. You have no choice – this is your mission. The Light goes to war with The Dark, once and for all.

It is when you take back the knowledge that was stolen, you may fight. Without it you are useless, a slave to The Dark. Our heavy and light bodies must be remembered and aligned and perfected before we can fight. The secret to doing this is in the symbolism of World War II.

You've been looking at The Swastika wrong. *Their* version of it is flat. In black, white and red. This makes it a logo akin to the McDonalds arch or the peanut with the top-hat and cane. This is misdirection.

It is really a three dimensional interactive diagram.

What it describes, in the simplest terms, is two counter-rotating movements of energy. This must be remembered and mastered, for this is how we switch on our other body. Our light body, our heavenly body.

To do this we must understand another symbol from World War II, The Star Of David. These two intersecting triangles are to be seen three dimensionally, not flat, with you in the middle. This is your vehicle to heaven.

On a flag you are looking at The Swastika from above. In reality, you look at it from the side, three dimensionally. When you do this, you'll see that the two intersecting S shapes are not touching, a great distance is between them. It is within this space you place your vehicle.

When you imagine yourself inside a three-dimensional Star Of David, your imagination charges the cardinal points of your energetic field, enabling you to move between worlds.

What the Swastika is trying to tell you, is to rotate the triangle pointing down to your right and the one pointing up to your left. These counter-rotating movements start the engine of your vehicle.

The symbol of The Swastika and The Star Of David are instructions on how to time travel.

The Bible Interpretor

We enter this scene as a substitute teacher gives his interpretation of Biblical stories and their meanings, in front of a gathering of uninterested students, wondering where they normal teacher is.

'The meek shall inherit the earth. You know that saying? The meek. Who are the meek? The meek have been thought of as: The Weak. That's easy, it rhymes. Nice easy correlation to make.: Meek/Weak.

And they who think of The Meek as The Weak are trying to say: The downtrodden will inherit the earth.

But what the word 'Meek' really means, is Humble. And some of the people who think of The Meek as The Weak, know that The Meek really means The Humble. But they still have a misunderstanding of the word Humble.

They think The Humble have seen the horrors of life and thought: OK, that's terrifying but I'm OK with it, because it's the way it's meant to be. And life will be how it's meant to be.

Again, this is a misunderstanding of language.

To be humble is not to just accept the version of life that is presented in front of your eyes, and say: Oh, that's OK. That's the way things go. That's just The Divine Plan playing itself out.

That is not humble, that is blind, two-fold blind.
First blinded by the world, then blinded by the
thing that told you the world was a lie. But by then
you were too terrified to take the final step...into
Truth. And most people are. This is why the world
is asleep, and they think the meek shall inherit the
earth.

I'm sure you know, when these people speak of
'The Meek' they are referring to themselves. The
Lambs Of God. The Blood Of Christ.

Little do they know they are God. They are Christ.
They are the lamb, and they are the blood. But one
thing they are not, is: The Meek.

Meek means humble. But not humbled *by* life,
humbled by *seeing* thee Light.
Because once you see thee Light, you will be one
humble motherfucker.
And until then 'The Meek' will sit in front of you,
swabbed in robes, burning incense, and saying
Namaste. Until you realize these motherfuckers
have been playing dress-up all along.

The Real Meek are the ones who went all the way.
And when you go all the way, you see the true face
of what people call God. And when you see that
face, you become humble. Not because you submit
to it, but because you remember you are it. You
always were it and always will be it.

The reflection you look at in the mirror is the face
of God reflecting back on itself.

Now do you realise why 'The Meek', do not flap
their lips of the other?

Annabella

Part 1.

Princess Annabella was one of seven sisters. She had the blondest of blonde hair, that hung like fragile crystal lace around her face, and through which the most perfect ears protruded. She had the bluest of blue eyes, that sat large and enquiring above a perfect regal nose and plump lips. Her wide cheek bones met at a delicate chin.

One day Princess Annabella gathered her family together. I want to go to Earth, she announced. Why would you want to go to Earth, her father laughed, did you not heed the stories I read you of that place?

Annabella, her mother interjected, you know how they treat our type on Earth, darling; With all the freedom we enjoy here, why would you want to go there?

I can't explain, said Annabella with a defiant stomp of her foot, but I've made up my mind, I'm going!

Princess Annabella came from a far-off place that did not know the hardships of Earth. The place she had come from lived in everlasting peace. People were not mean to each other. They did not betray one another. No one hurt anyone else and everyone told the truth. The word No did not exist, for there was no reason for it to exist.

Princess Annabella had heard of the place called

Earth, from stories her father would read to her as a little girl. She had recoiled at the tales of struggle and sorrow and sadness. She could not comprehend that people could live like this.

Father, she said, how can these people not see the oppression they live under? Why did these people, who lived on Earth, not do anything about it? Did they not want to be free?

Maybe, her father replied, they had never known freedom or knew they wanted it. Maybe they thought they were free all along, so never fought for it.

It makes me sick to my tummy, to think people live like that, said Annabella. One day I wish for everyone to live as we do.

And I do too Annabella, replied her father. But it is up to the people of Earth to free themselves.

Annabella frowned, One day I will help the people of Earth be free father.

Her father laughed and bid her a safe journey. You must follow your heart, he whispered in her ear, as they embraced, but please be careful!

The first night Annabella arrived on Earth she went to a funfair. She walked amongst the heaving masses, tall and slender and elegant.

She watched boys and girls in each others arms. They laughed and hugged and kissed, and displayed all the gestures one does when in love. But it did not seem real to Annabella. It was like they were pretending to be in love. Like they had been told: This is how you act when you are in love. And so the boys and girls just acted being in love. It was not real love.

Where Annabella came from, people really loved each other. In total freedom. Here it seemed like the boys and girls where only together, because they were missing a part of themselves, which they thought the other person could make up for.

Annabella watched a girl slap her boyfriend on the face, because he had looked at a group of passing girls. Why is he not allowed to look at other girls? she laughed. They are beautiful.

She watched a boy start a fight with a group of other boys, because they had looked at his girlfriend. Why does he care if other boys look at his girlfriend? She is beautiful.

As Annabella walked around the funfair she looked at all the rides. All the screaming people on them, scaring themselves into hysterical laughter. What an odd place, she thought.

The smell of candyfloss and popcorn and hot-dogs filled Annabella's nose, smells she had never smelt before. The screams and laughs and mechanical pumping of the machinery filled her ears. What an experience for the senses, she thought.

As she passed a hall of mirrors she saw a young girl sitting by herself on a bench. The girl had no boyfriend and was gazing into nothingness like there was something there.

Annabella approached, and sat beside her.

The girl didn't move.

Hello, said Annabella.
The girl did not react.
Hi, Annabella said, placing a hand on the girls thigh.
The girls gaze shifted from looking at nothingness, to looking at Annabella's hand on her thigh, then to Annabella's face.
Still she said nothing.

Are you OK? Asked Annabella.
Do you really care if I'm OK, came the detached reply.
Yes, said Annabella, why would I not care.
Why would you care? Answered the girl.
Because you seem like the most honest person here, said Annabella.

The girl snorted back a mock laugh.

Honest, I'm fucking depressed. Can't you tell?
Yes, that's why you're the most honest person here. That's why I was drawn to you, because you are not hiding how you truly feel inside. I think it's beautiful.

What's beautiful about being depressed, the girl half asked.
It's not the depression that is beautiful, it's your

bravery in displaying it, and not pretending you're happy. That makes you the most honest person here, replied Annabella. You know Truth.

The girl wrinkled her forehead: And you're the strangest person here.

Thank you, said Annabella.

The girl looked away in puzzled amusement.

I was wondering if you could tell me the most fun ride I could go on. Asked Annabella. I'm not from around here and would like to experience this place in its purest form.

You should go in the ghost train, the girl pointed. Loads of fun in there.

Thank you very much, Annabella replied.

With that she stood and walked in the direction the girl had pointed. A train of carts awaited at a rickety old station. Red smoke leaked from a set of black doors they faced. Skeletons and hovering white sheets cackled and gasped at her, demonically. Annabella laughed and walked towards them.

How much is this ride? she asked the man at the kiosk.

Free to you madam, pick a cart and it will begin shortly.

Thank you, said Annabella.

She walked up the platform. Counting seven empty carts, she chose the first one, right at the front. A whirring, whirling and maniacal song began to play as the train jolted forwards. Annabella grasped the handrail, giggling in shock.

Her cart trundled along the tracks, towards the set of black doors leaking red smoke. As she bumped through them, the smoke engulfed her. She coughed and waved it away. As the seventh cart entered, the doors slammed shut and she was in total darkness.

As Annabella's eyes adjusted, she saw the walls undulating in deep red and black like they were alive. A hypnotic thump, droned all around her. Boom boom, boom boom. The low frequencies vibrated deep in her bones.

The temperature seemed to switch in an instant, and sweat gathered on her brow as her hands and feet became clammy. Fanning her face, Annabella blew cool air into the atmosphere around her, but she only got warmer.

The train picked up speed. Annabella grasped the guardrail with both hands. The hypnotic thump grew louder and faster, until it seemed she was submerged in it.
Boom boom boom boom boom boom boom.

Sweat beaded down her face from raw fear, a wholly new sensation to her.

A blinding white light brought her focus straight ahead. The train raced towards it. She braced herself against the brightness, as she exploded into it.

Part 2.
Annabella felt drowsy and heavy. She watched the darkness behind her eyelids. Her head hung to her chest, her body suspended, a high-pitched ringing in her ears. Her vision was blurred and shifting, as she slowly opened her eyes.

Where am I, and what happened? she thought.

She was chained to a wall, her arms and legs stretched, shackled in the shape of a star. The cell was nine-foot square. There was a door in front of her, and another to her right. They were identical with a small, barred window, just above eye level.

The interior of the cell was red and black. A patchwork of primitive technology covered the walls, it seemed so ancient it looked futuristic. The locking mechanisms on the doors were complex, baffling and entirely alien to her.

For the first time in her life Princess Annabella screamed.

And then she screamed again.

And once more, a scream so wretched it cut the back of her throat and she spat blood.

The door in front of her clicked and groaned.

Smoothly it opened to show a hooded figure standing there. A black hooded robe over a large body, showing only black boots and the face shadowed. A right hand peaked through a sleeve, scarred red and a glinting silver claw where the left hand should have been.

The figure approached Annabella in silence.

Why are you doing this to me? she croaked.

Why did you come into my house, if you did not want this to happen dear Annabella? replied the figure, with a voice thin and sinuous.

I was at the funfair and wanted to experience this ride. I didn't know what it was.

Yes, this is what happens when you get on that ride my dear. Before you know it you're trapped in the world of The Black Magician, who is I. And now that I have you here, I want three things from you.

I don't have anything with me, Annabella cried.

You have everything I need my dear. I want your ears, your nose and your eyes.

Annabella screamed.

The Black Magician laughed.

Now dear, he said coming face to face with her, which shall I take first. Annabella struggled. The Black Magician restrained her, his claw slicing her left arm.

Now, now dear. The more you fight the worse it will be.

I've never had to fight before, wept Annabella, noticing the blood trickling from her arm.

Exactly, so why start now.

Annabella looked at The Black Magician through her tears. He removed his hood.

His head and face were completely shaved. Deep furrows lined his forehead. Large grey bags under small dark inset eyes. Purple lips on the brink of foaming madness. Acne marks indented his cheeks. A large scar through his left eyebrow. His white skin, puffy and sagging.

May I take your ears first, he spit-whispered.

Annabella looked at him in confusion. She did not want him to take her ears, but having never been asked such a horrendous question before, she did not know how to reply.

Think about it while I sharpen my knife, he said turning away. Delving a hand into the robe The Black Magician pulled out a blade that was equally razor-sharp and obsidian-black. He walked to a wall where a strap hung. As he swiped the blade back and forth on it, he eyed Annabella from the side.

Well, may I cut off your ears? He asked.

Annabella did not know how to tell someone not to do something. She had no language for it. She stared at him distressed, her body convulsing in tremors.

Where she came from if someone wanted something you just give it to them, knowing what was meant for you will come from that act of kindness.

OK, she barely said.

With a lunge forward, The Black Magician swiped at the left side of her head. The top of her ear sailed through the air, wisps of blonde hair followed. Dark red blood shot forth from the wound, matting her hair in thick clumps, and flowing down her neck.

She squeezed her eyes shut in terror, as the pain turned from numbness to excruciating. Ahhhhhhhhh, she gritted through her teeth, her head dropping to her chest once more. So this is what pain feels like, she thought.

The Black Magician laughed, grasping her in a headlock, he brought the blade to her throat. Now for this one, he said, separating her hair, with his clawed hand, exposing the other ear.

With that he sunk his teeth into it, shaking his head like a feral cat killing a mouse, gnawing until Annabella's ear came off in his mouth. He held it between his teeth, giggling like a child.

Blood poured down Annabella's left side, as The Black Magician lifted her head up by her hair. Her eyes rolled, as she moved in and out of consciousness.

The last thing she saw was The Black Magician's blood smeared giggling face, with her ear between his teeth, before she passed out.

Part 3.
The White Magician was standing in his bathroom, looking at his reflection in the mirror. His matted hair reached his elbows, in long dreadlocks, each as unique as the other. He had never had it cut. His long, grey beard swung over his chest. It was his pride and joy, and he took many hours shaping, grooming and oiling it to perfection.

The White Magician knew his body hair to be an outward expression of his nervous system. That's why he took such care of it.

Gazing into his eyes through the bathroom mirror, The White Magician clicked the electric shaver on. It buzzed in his hand. He brought it to just below his jawline, on the right side, and with a deep breath, pushed upwards. It sheared through his beard on his right cheek, up past his ear, and onto the side of his head.

He pushed further, as long ropes of hair fell around him. He pushed on to the crown, finishing at his left ear, his hair dropped on its maiden voyage to the ground, like the feathers of an angel who had just been shot.

He brought the electric shaver to eye level and blew at the blades, to clear them. Then he followed the exact mirror opposite journey, from below his jawline on the left side, to behind his ear on the right. The ground accepted its payload with coy abandon.

Then he moved from his forehead to the back of his neck. The electric shaver vibrating his skull as he did so. Then his chin. Then his moustache. Then his eyebrows.

Standing in a heap of black and grey hair, The White Magician's reflection was unrecognisable to him. He looked like a nasty piece of work now. Just the right disguise to infiltrate The Black Magician's labyrinth.

Part 4.
Annabella pried her eyes open. Hardened blood had sealed then shut. Her blue and white dress now painted in dark red smears. She wanted to collapse, but all she could do was let the shackles take her weight as she hung from them. Her skinned wrists and ankles were scraped raw from the metal.

Ah, she awakens, came the words from approaching footsteps. Well not quite, still a little sleepy, laughed The Black Magician, raising her head with his claw under her chin.

He stared into her eyes saying nothing.

Then broke the silence: Annabella, I know you came here with a mission to destroy me...

I didn't come here to destroy anything, Annabella interrupted, I only want to experience this place...

And that is the experience you are getting, dear Annabella, said The Black Magician, gesturing to the cell.

Now I think I'd like to take your nose next. Is that alright with you? He asked.

Why would you want to do that, she snapped. Why would you let me, he snapped back.

Annabella fell silent again.

Poor Annabella, The Black Magician laughed, it's so easy if you only knew how. But you wanted the experience, so let me give you the experience.

He pulled the razor sharp obsidian blade from his hooded robe and inserted the tips of his clawed hand in each of Annabella's nostrils. Stretching them up and out.

Annabella wept heaving tears. So this is what terror feels like, she thought, remembering the stories her father had read to her as a child.

Well? Can I have your nose? He asked.

Not knowing how to refuse him, the letters OK, fell from her lips.

Part 5.
The White Magician arrived at the funfair, as hairless as the day he was born. Wearing black boots, black jeans, a black shirt, black denim jacket and a black beanie pulled low on his face.

He manoeuvred around the throngs of people, finally locating the ghost train. Walking up to the man in the kiosk, he dropped the coins into his hand, saying: One please.

Go right ahead sir, the man said motioning to the train.

The White Magician sat in the last of seven carts, so he could get a good view. Exhaling a deep sigh, he relaxed a little. Rubbing his hands, he placed them gently on the guardrail before him.

He sat waiting for the ride to start, as red smoked creaked out of the black doors facing the front of the train. He looked over to the man in the kiosk, raising his shoulders to his ears, and eyebrows upwards.

Just a minute sir, kiosk man replied, having some technical difficulties. Won't be a moment.

The White Magician returned his gaze to the black doors for what seemed like forever. Suddenly the train jerked, and moved forward, the first cart banging the doors open. Plumes of red smoke burst forth, as one by one, the carts entered. Here we go, he said under his breath.

As the last cart entered, the doors slammed shut and The White Magician was bathed in darkness. He closed his eyes, breathed deep and braced himself.

He heard the sound of running feet. The sound was coming towards him. All of a sudden he felt his movement restricted, as a sack was roughly pulled over his head. It tightened at the opening, around his waist, as he was tied into it. The rope cutting into his belly and halting his breath, his arms tight against his ribs.

He felt a pressure on the back of his neck, as someone held something to it. He heard the zap of high electricity, and a searing pain sent his body into convulsions. As he seizured helplessly inside the sack, he lost consciousness.

Part 6.
Annabella stared down at her feet lifelessly. Her legs lined with rivers of dried blood, connected to the congealed pool around her limp hanging body. She turned in her eyes to see the bloody stump where her nose was.

She coughed out a slimy clot from her throat, spitting it with as much force as she could muster, as if that clot contained all the anger she felt, and, until this very moment, had never felt before.

Is this the experience people come here for? she thought.

She shook her head, to try and bring herself around a little. As she did, she noticed strands of hair falling around her, gently floating into the blood at her feet, without a care in the world.

She cried.

Part 7.
The rumble of bass and drums shook The White Magician awake. As he slowly came to they grew louder. He was still tied into the sack, slumped and half seated. He was aware of the presence of many people around him.

They think I'm dead, he thought.

He felt the jut of elbows, and the slamming of thighs into his body. As his hearing attuned to his surroundings, he realised he was in the heart of a nightclub. The music blasted from speakers loud enough that the people around him had to shout to be heard. The clink of glasses and throaty laughter. He inhaled and the smell of alcohol, smoke and dry ice filled his nostrils.

At least I'm alive, he thought, and by the sounds of it, inside The Labyrinth of The Black Magician. Now, he wondered, when is the best time to let them know I'm not dead?

Part 8.

A swash of cold water brought Annabella around from the fog of inertia.

Wake up!

The Black Magician was seated in front of her. She heard muffled clicks, each one syncopated and direct.

Time, The Black Magician said pointing to a clock on the wall that wasn't there before.

I've bought you some time, he laughed. Me and time are best friends you see, dear Annabella. Let me tell you a story.

Annabella exhaustedly listened as well as her blood filled ears would allow.

When I first came here it was beautiful. And I met the most beautiful woman you could imagine, she ruled the land. She was so free and loving and open. She feared nothing. But, I could not have this. I had to have control over her. So I married her. I became Mr and she became Mr's. She was Mine, imprisoned within the joys of matrimony.

One day I decided to lock her in a room. With nothing but a ticking clock. The sound of that clock was like a blade into her consciousness. One day she went totally insane. Her problem was, she was too naïve. She had never experienced any of the horrors I was subjecting her to and she didn't know how to react.

Now, I ruled the land. And I made it law that anyone who came to my land, would live under my rule. And that rule was that every house would have a ticking clock. I have many many many people under my rule now. They have been for so long, they don't remember a time when they were not, a time when they were free. A time before time.

And it all started with me. This old, out of shape white man, dressed in a hooded robe with a claw for a hand. Little old me. And believe me, I am old.

The ticking of the clock PECK-PECKED relentlessly in Annabelle's bloody ear holes.

One day I boarded up the windows in my wife's room, the Black Magician continued. I denied her the presence of any light, and for the rest of her days she lived in darkness.

I would shout through the door: Dear wife, dear wife. Is there anything you would like to tell me?

But like an obedient spouse, she didn't answer. She had no word for what I was really asking her. So I let her rot and decay, deprived of light.

One day, I heard on the grapevine that she had borne a son, before we had met. And he was coming to save her. This made me furious. The thought of her having sex with anyone else, never mind producing a brat from that union, threw me into a blind rage.

That night I entered her room. Her pathetic corpse of a body, huddled in the corner. I have heard you have been a naughty girl, I said to her.

I could not have this. So I cut off her ears. Cut off her nose. And scooped her eyeballs out of her sockets.

And that brings us up to right now, dear Annabella. For what I will take from you next, is your eyes. If that is alright of course. But I'm sure if it's not, you'll let me know.

Annabella barely spoke: What happened to your wife?

She is still rotting in her room, awaiting her son to save her. You are not the first girl I've had down here Annabella, believe me.

Why do you do this, said Annabella trying to understand.

Because it's just who I am, replied The Black Magician, it's what my character does.

Part 8.
The White Magician carefully slipped his fingers under the sack and untied the knot locking him in. As it fell away he felt the rope loosen from his waist. He took a deep breath in, for what felt like the first time in forever.

It's now or never, he thought.

Grasping the sides of the sack between his fingers, he quickly pulled it off, like a rabbit out of a hat.

Time slowed down.

He was in an opened cubicle, seated on a red leather semi-circular seat. Two henchmen to his left, two to his right, and one sat on a separate chair in front of him. They were all black with dreadlocks hanging down their faces. They looked at him in shock. Like he had just risen from the dead. He looked down at the table and saw five different pistols amongst the drinks and ashtrays.

The silence was louder than the blasting music around them.

The White Magician held the gaze of the henchman directly in front of him. He seemed to be the top dog here.

He had a one chance to perform magic before all hell broke loose. He had to keep their nervous systems in a state of surprise, then with electromagnetic magic suspend it there, giving him time to survey the scene and get to the cells.

My nigga, he said fist bumping the henchman in front of him. The Henchman didn't know whether to be offended or laugh or kill this idiot.

The White Magician turned to the henchman at his right: What up fam!
The henchman wide eyed him. Turning to look at his comrades. They all put their eyes back on The

White Magician in silent surprise. This was the moment.

He pushed out an electromagnetic pulse from his thymus gland in the shape of a sphere, encapsulating everyone around the table in it. This froze their emotions from the time it touched them. Suspended in time, but unaware of it.

Inside this sphere it was silent, The White Magician telepathically suggested to the men: I'm your friend, we're all just having a drink and a laugh. You've all known me as long as each other. I'm just like you.

The White Magician coughed. And time began again. The music of the dancefloor blasted back into life.

Everyone at the table snapped out of the suspension and continued like they had known The White Magician forever. Drinks slammed, cigarettes smoked, and conversations intersected each other.

The White Magician surveyed the surroundings. He was indeed inside a club. Cubicles littered the left side, filled with henchmen drinking and laughing. A long bar, packed with people waiting to be served, stretched from the left side wall to the start of the dancefloor that filled the right side of the room. Small podiums were dotted about the dancefloor, where girls gyrated against poles that reached to the ceiling.

The White Magician eyed the girls more closely. They were all various tones of black, with bruised skin and deformed bones. Slave girls of The Black Magician. Like the henchmen were slave boys to The Black Magician.

The day they realise what he's really doing, is the day they are free, he thought.

His eyes moved to the front of the dancefloor. A small stage arose. And there sitting on a throne of bones was The Black Magician himself. A fat hairless old white man. Dressed in black and drinking from a goblet made from a gilded skull, while his slave girls danced for him.

He slapped their bottoms, threw money at them, and generally humiliated them.

The White Magician spied a doorway at the side of the dancefloor. If he could just get to it, he could navigate his way to the cells underground.

He rose from the circular seat, patting a henchman on the shoulder like they were old friends. He motioned that he was going to the toilet. He stepped over their legs, and out of the cubicle.

He walked down a few steps and made his way through the dancefloor. Pulling his hat low on his face to avoid detection, he fingered an electrical burn on the back of his neck. As he snaked pass the dancing people, he kept glancing up at The Black Magician, to see if he had been noticed. He hadn't.

The door was on a raised stage that ran around the perimeter of the club. Once he stood up there, he was in full view of everyone. He kept checking The Black Magician, waiting for him to divert his eyes in the other direction.

Luckily a dancing slave girl was beckoned for a personal lap dance. She wrapped her legs around him, pushing her breasts in his face. Perfect, now's the time.

The White Magician stepped up to the door and pulled it towards him. But it didn't budge. It was locked. The locking mechanisms were so ancient they seemed futuristic. Nothing he had seen before. As he started to work them, he heard a shout. He looked to The Black Magician and saw him make a sign with his hand, to the group of henchmen in the cubicle. They snapped out of their trance as The Black Magician clicked his fingers, and motioned to kill this intruder.

The White Magician panicked, as the club turned to chaos around him. The Black Magician threw off the dancing slave girl from his lap. She hit the ground with a thud. She had had enough. She stood up and slapped The Black Magician hard. He grabbed her by her throat and started strangling her.

The dancing slave girls left their podiums and pounced on The Black Magician, tearing at him with nails, teeth and heels.

Another group made their way towards The White

Magician. I'm done for he thought. But they created a barrier around him with their bodies. To buy him more time before the henchmen could get to him.

The White Magician navigated the locks. The henchmen where right behind him, beating their way through the girls who shielded him. Finally, a lock popped open. He pulled the door towards him, entered, and slammed it shut. The mechanism automatically locking it.

He took a moment to breathe and listened to the chaos on the otherside.

The White Magician turned and was confronted with a hall of mirrors. He stepped into it, but every step he took, the mirrors shifted position. They doubled, then trebled, then quadrupled. The floor was mirrored now. Then the ceiling too. The structure closed in on him until the image of a thousand faces looking back at him, made him scream in such terror, he passed out.

Part 9.
Annabella. Annabella. Dear, Annabella: The Black Magician sang.

Annabella raised her head to see The Black Magician sat in front of her again. He had a silver spoon on his hand that was not a claw.

He was seated with his legs wide apart. His black hooded robe hanging like a canopy between his knees. She noticed he was bare foot, for the first time without his heavy boots.

Annabella, I would like to show you the source of all my power. You just hang there and watch. If I see you close your eyes, I will use this spoon to scoop them out. Do you understand?

Annabella nodded weakly. She heard a thump in her right ear. Followed by another two. Her eye tweaked in spasm.

The Black Magician slowly pulled up his robe. Exposing his legs, mapped in varicose veins and age spots. He pulled it higher past his knees, deformed with arthritis.

Annabella swallowed hard, her throat dry and aching.

He continued, pulling his robe up to his waist she saw his flaccid penis hanging lifelessly against old, elongated testicles. It was black and mutilated with time. Warts and growths and spiderwebs filled his inner thighs. Gnarled grey hairs sprouted everywhere, thick and singed.

She vomited acidic green bile which dripped from her chin as she tried to spit it out.

The Black Magician laughed.

She looked into his eyes.

He motioned for her to look back at his genitals, slowly waving the spoon.

As she brought her eyes back down, his penis

started to become engorged. It folded away from his testicles, and rose upwards. Pulsing purple veins hugged the shaft, as it become erect his foreskin pulled back, exposing a diseased looking head.

Annabella stifled more vomit.

And that, dear Annabella, is the source of all my power. He calmly said.

Would you like to touch it? He stood pulling his robe completely off. His large belly hanging and sagging pectorals hung low. He started a slow walk towards her.

Or maybe give it a kiss?

Annabella felt a pressure in her heart. It felt like the love she had once known before visiting Earth, but why was she feeling this when this horrendous ordeal was taking place.

Then her head took control. She stared at The Black Magician in confusion.

He came face to face with her and pressed his naked body against her.

Maybe I can put it inside you, he whispered before roughly kissing her, delving his tongue into her bloody bile dripping mouth.

You taste so good, he whimpered.

He stood back and with one swipe of his claw cut Annabelle's dress in half. It fell open, exposing her blood stained naked body. She tried crossing her legs as much as the shackles would allow, but it was useless.

The Black Magician stood back and started masturbating.

Annabella closed her eyes tightly. The Black Magician lunged at her, grabbing her head, he used his claw to pry her left eye open, and plunged the spoon in, digging it out in scooping motions until it was hanging on her cheek. He took it between his teeth and ripped it from the stems.

Annabella's body went limp as she passed out into total unconsciousness.

Part 10.
The White Magician came to, lying on a dirt floor. Muffled voices echoed from somewhere above his head. He gathered his bearings, and sat up. The room was decorated in ancient black and red technology which seemed sentient.

The White Magician brought his gaze higher. A small door to his right. A small bed in front of him. To his left a broken mirror high on the wall. Beside that a larger door with a barred window. Behind him a blank wall with only a speaker hanging from it.

He turned and stared at the speaker. His head swam with muffled voices as full consciousness returned and his ears attuned to his surroundings. The voices were coming from the speaker.

He stood, tilting his neck up to hear better. A crackling voice was speaking:

Annabella, I would like to show you the source of all my power. You just hang there and watch. If I see you close your eyes, I will use this spoon to scoop them out. Do you understand?

Annabella! The White Magician exclaimed. He looked to his right at the door with the barred window. Running to it, he thumped the glass once, feeling it's thickness. He then thumped it twice again.

Looking through the window he saw Annabella chained to a wall, her body stretched out like a star. The Black Magician was sat in front of her, in his hooded robe but barefoot, holding a silver spoon in the hand that was not a claw.

Annabella! The White Magician screamed.

His own voice reverberated around the room. It was soundproof, but The Black Magician was piping in the sounds from Annabella's cell, so The White Magician could hear everything.

The White Magician sat back down on the floor. Crossed his legs and closed his eyes. He brought his full awareness to the breath entering and leaving his nostrils. The sounds from the adjoining room slowly fell away as he went inwards.

He then preformed a technique known as The Breath of Death. It was a technique only known to the most advanced of magicians. A technique that allows one to leave the body at will.

He breathed in for three seconds, out for five and retained his breath until he left his body.

The White Magician's body seizured as he stepped out of it. He had done it. He was in the invisible realm that plays out concurrent with the realm people know as reality. The invisible realm is not ruled by the constructs of the reality realm, but only people who have learnt this could interact with it.

The White Magician approached the door with the barred window, and walked right through it. He stood in Annabella's cell, watching The Black Magician pull off his robe and walk towards Annabella.

...or maybe give it a kiss, he heard him say to her.

The Black Magician was too involved in the torture to sense an astral version of The White Magician was in his presence.

The White Magician walked towards Annabella and placed his hand on her heart. He felt it beat with a purity unknown to most people on Earth. He placed his mouth to her right ear and whispered: Just Say No.

He stepped back and watched The Black Magician roughly kissing her, then ripping her dress off with his clawed hand, before walking through the wall and back into his body.

As he gradually came back into the realm of reality, The White Magician ran to the barred window again. He watched as The Black Magician started masturbating in front of Annabella.

Don't close your eyes, he screamed. But the words went unheard, as he watched Annabella close her eyes and The Black Magician gouge one out. He diverted his gaze as he saw The Black Magician gnawing at the stems.

His heart sunk. What else could he do. She hadn't heard him speak through dimensions into her heart.

He looked through the window again to see her lifeless body, hanging in unconsciousness. He banged on the barred window with both fists making as much noise as possible.

He watched through the window as The Black Magician reared his head towards him.

Silly boy, he heard piped through the speaker, you will never save her now. I have her where I want her. Subservient to my power. I could end it all now, if only she could tell me. But she can't and won't.

The White Magician banged on the window with a flurry of fists.
The Black Magician ran towards to opposing door,

laughing maniacally. He grabbed the bars and shook them, shaking his head like a wild beast, putrid tongue bared and slabbering.

Annabella came too, vomited blood from her mouth, and excreted a mixture of blood and shit down her legs.

The White and Black Magician looked at her at the same time.

Ah, our darling Annabella is awakening, The White Magician heard The Black Magician say through the speaker, as he made his way towards her.

The White Magician rained down fists upon the barred glass window. Just say no, he screamed. Just say no!

Annabella heard the distance thumps and looked to her right. Through the small glass window she could see a man. He franticly banged at the glass, which produced only muffled thumps. He was mouthing words she couldn't decipher.

Ignore him Annabella, he is not to be trusted, The Black Magician said.

The man behind the glass was mouthing a large O shape with his lips. Who was he, she thought, and what's he trying to tell me.

The Black Magician grasped Annabella by the throat: Ignore him, he seethed through his rotten teeth at her.

With his clawed hand, The Black Magician
unlocked Annabelle's shackles. Manoeuvring the
tip like a key. She fell to the floor in a heap. He
grabbed her by the waist and positioned her on all
fours like a dog. His large belly swayed against her
lower back.

Now Annabella, I'm going to make you mine. This
is your last chance. So I ask you, will you allow me
to make you mine?

Annabella looked to the window of the adjoining
room, but no one was there.

Part 11.
The White Magician scanned the room. Then he
brought his gaze upwards to the broken mirror,
high on the left wall beside the door. He jumped
up and punched it with the side of his fist, loose
shards fell to the floor.

Taking one, he dug it deep into his left arm and
dragged it across. The blood started to spurt. He
let it gather into a dripping pool on the floor and
sunk his first and second fingers into it.

Running back to the door, in a sway of light
headedness, he wrote the letters N O on the glass
backwards. And started thumping it with all his
strength, as the blood for his arm hit the walls in
abstract slashes.

Part 12.
Annabella could feel the diseased head of The
Black Magician's penis at the opening of her

vagina. She vomited more bile into her hands which were pressing against the floor caked in her own blood.

She looked to the window again. This time she saw two letters, written in dripping red. She read them in her mind: N. O.

These formations of sound made her remember the pressure she had felt in her heart, when it had told her a word that she had never uttered before.

Well Annabella, what is your answer, may I make you mine? The Black Magician laughed, as he started to insert his penis into her vagina.

NO!!!!!! Annabella screamed.
The Black Magician recoiled, falling back on his heels.
Annabella turned, a huddled mess.
NO!!!!!!!! She screamed at his face.

The Black Magician struggled to his feet. Searching for his robe he threw it over his body, placing the hood over his head.

Annabella rose to her feet, a starved bloody mess. She walked towards The Black Magician as he stepped back, knocking over the chair.

Annabella took a deep breath in and felt her heartbeat rise. In all her nakedness, she stared The Black Magician deep in his eyes and from the bottom of her stomach screamed: NO!!!!!!!!!!!!

The Black Magician convulsed under his robes. His body shaking in tremors. His face started to melt away like sand running down an hourglass. His hooded robe shrunk as it caved in on itself.

Annabella heard a clunk and saw his claw hit the ground, as his right hand reached out to her, turning to sand and falling to a pile on the floor. In an instant, The Black Magician's robe totally deflated and lay in a heap on top of a pile of sand with a claw jutting out if it.

A slow mechanical turning sound came from the doors, as they slowly opened. With the demise of The Black Magician, The Labyrinth unlocked itself. She looked out at the hallway in front of her, then turned to the right to see a man lying in a pool of blood, through the adjoining door.

She ran to him.

I think I cut a bit deep, he said showing her his left wrist, but at least you got the message. Now if it's OK with you, I'm going to pass out. The man passed out.

The White Magician awoke to gentle slaps on his face, and a low murmuring voice: Come on, come on, come on. It was saying.

He pealed his eyes open.

You were so still, I thought you were dead: Annabella said to the awakening White Magician. No, not yet. Must be more work to do, he laughed.

She pulled him up by his left arm. Ouch, he said as Annabella looked down at his bleeding wrist.

Sorry, she said.
Don't worry about it. What's a little blood between friends? he replied, shaking his arm.

The White Magician looked at Annabella. She was naked except for the blood that covered her body. Her left eye closed over in a swollen lump. Her nose a bloody stump. Her ears nothing but holes in the side of her head. Her hair all but fallen out.

He took off his denim jacket, wrapped it around her and hugged her tightly.

How did you know where I was, she said into the pit of his neck.

Those of pure heart can talk with a language beyond words, he replied. A language most people on Earth are not aware of. Where you are from you know this language. But in order to visit Earth you must forget it. Then, hopefully while you're here, remember it again.

Annabella wrinkled her brow. What a strange man, she thought.

Let's get you home, The White Magician said.

As they walked from the room, into Annabella's cell, he saw the pile of sand, with a hooded robe on top and silver claw jutting out. He walked towards it. Squatting down, he picked up the robe and hugged it. Nice to meet you brother, he whispered to it.

Dropping it back into the sand, he took Annabella by the hand, and they walked out of the cell.

She was confronted by a never-ending hallway, filled with cells on each side. She went to run to one. The White Magician grabbed her arm.

No Annabella, you are not here to save the people in those cells. You only had to save yourself. And look, where is The Black Magician now? He is nothing but a pile of sand. These doors have been unlocked. But the people inside must choose for themselves when to walk out of them. The word you screamed is their key to freedom too. But you must let them say it themselves.

Annabella hugged the man tightly.
Why did you do this for me, she asked.
It's just who I am, he replied, shrugging his shoulders. It's what my character does.

They walked out of The Labyrinth of The Black Magician back into the funfair. It was empty and quiet. The sun was just rising to bathe Earth in his light.

Annabella looked at her reflection in the glass of the kiosk. Expecting to see a horror-show looking back at her, she saw that her nose and ears and eyes were perfect. Her hair thick and abundant. She looked down and was wearing the same dress, clean from blood, that she had worn when she first arrived.

You see, The White Magician said pointing to the
ghost train, It was just a ride.

What will happen to The Black Magician's wife?
Annabella asked. She is still locked in that room.
Are you not free, The White Magician replied.
Huh? Annabella shrugged.

Have you ever heard the stories of the planets? He
asked
My father would read me many stories of the
planets as a child, she replied.
Ah, the planets of Earth I meant, The White
Magician said. In our story the son, he pointed to
himself, always frees the mother, he pointed to her,
from the oppressive father, he pointed to his
genitals.

Annabella laughed: You are so strange.
Thank you, replied The White Magician as he
turned to walk away.

But however can I repay you, Annabella shouted.

What's meant for you will always come to you, he
replied in a half turn.
What's meant for you will always come to you, he
repeated to himself.
Hopefully my hair, he shouted rubbing his bald
head.

What do I do now, Annabella called to his
retreating figure.

Go home Annabella, The White Magician said
without turning around, go home.

The Cleaner

The Cleaner cleaned houses. He cleaned them not for money, but for a meal after each day of work.

The Cleaner was an old man. He had lived a good life. Now retired, he still wanted to be of service. So, one day he put an advert in his local shop:

Cleaner Available.
'No Haus Too Dirty'
Phone or Text: +09 1255102

The Cleaner made his own all purpose cleaner:
½ cup of water.
½ cup of white vinegar.
2 tablespoons of baking soda.
10 drops of lemon and lime juice.

He placed this in a small, wooden caddy with wheels, along with:

A collection of home made cloths, cut from the t-shirts he would wear in his youth. These were of various bands he released when he owned a record label, their 40 year old logos now being reused to clean with.

A wooden scrubber that was once a beard brush. The same brush he had used on his mighty beard for many years. The Cleaner had decided to never shave again in his youth when he started growing a beard. Now an old man, he preferred the cleanly-shaved look.

A scented candle. Which he made himself and lit at the end of each cleaning session in the client's home.

The Stepmother Pt. 1
The Cleaner stood at the door of a new client's town house, holding the handle of his wooden caddy containing his cleaning products. He looked at a small home-made sign hanging in the window: Leave Yo' Drama Wit' Yo' Mama, it read. He chuckled, knowing that this house would be filled with nothing but drama.

He pushed the doorbell, which didn't work, then used the letterbox, which snapped aggressively back at him. After a cascade of thumping footsteps downstairs, a blustering woman answered. Dark eyes nearly black in the dim light of the hallway.

I'm The Cleaner, he said.
Good, come in, come in.
She shook his hand firmly, too firmly
She wants me to know she's the one in control here, he thought.
I like your sign, he said pointing to it in the window.
Ah yes. Everyone is welcome here, but their bullshit is not, she replied.

He laughed.

I've got a few friends over, we're having a drink in the living room. I'll show you about, so you can get a feel for the place.

As they moved from room to room, she apologised for the mess, explaining she had taken the task of looking after her recently departed husband's son from his first marriage. Along with her own children, she also had a full-time job. So, no time to clean unfortunately.

I'm sorry for your loss Madam, The Cleaner said.

Less of the Madam, you make me sound ancient. No condolences needed. We had been separated for years. He was dead to me the day he walked out on his family.

A fiery lady, this one, thought The Cleaner, her words will burn her house down if she's not careful.

After the tour of the inside, she led him to the back yard. A small, paved area with an array of potted plants around the perimeter.

We keep the dog in the garden, she told him, pointing to a kennel. He has shit everywhere, she enraged.

Cookie! She screamed, at an unnecessary volume. Why can you not shit when I take you out for a walk. Why do you wait to do it here?

Turning to The Cleaner: I'm sorry about this.

A floppy eared Beagle's face slowly emerged from the kennel.

Coookieee. The Cleaner sang, slapping his thighs. The dog ran to him, jumping up as they met. The Cleaner held the dog's paws and squatted down to be level with him.

Oh you're such a sweetie Cookie, The Cleaner baby-talked to the dog. As sweet as a cookie even, he laughed. Looking up to the lady, he saw his joke had gone unnoticed.

Cookie rolled over and The Cleaner scratched his tummy. The dog's bright red penis suddenly made an appearance. Coming out like a lipstick, twisting free amongst his white and tan fur.

Put that filthy thing away, the lady said stamping her foot. The angry vibration causing Cookie to flee back to the safety of his kennel, penis retracting.

Sorry about that, she apologised.

Well it is her dog, thought The Cleaner saying nothing.

So, he said breaking the tension, I'll start in the kitchen.

The Teacher Pt. 1
The Cleaner was in a block of flats. The décor was 20 years out of date. He had made his way up two flights of stairs, his caddy bumping on each step behind him. He stood in front of wired glass doors. Level 3, a pealing yellow decal said.

His feeling was that the majority of people who lived here, were in a transitory period of their lives. Either between homes, between marriages or between old age and death.

He pushed the heavy doors open and located number thirteen. Checking the scrap of paper he had brought with him with the address on it, he knocked the door in three moderate raps, and waited.

Oh hello, you must be the cleaner, a small giggling woman said between the cracked doorway. One green eye, and one glass green eye. Come in, come.

The door didn't open all the way, and he squeezed in sidewards. Behind it, there were packing boxes filled with unknown mysteries, blocking it's full movement.

The hallway was tiny, and the lady who had answered the door stood breasts to chest with The Cleaner.

Just moved in Madam? The Cleaner asked.

She looked momentarily shocked, as if she wasn't good enough for such a title.

Yeah, but not staying long. No point unpacking if I'll be moving on soon, she replied.

People always think what's coming next is what's best for them, he thought, never seeing that the moment they are in is absolutely perfect.

Of course, he answered.

The woman explained that she was a music teacher. She had just split up with her husband and he had got the house. She was staying here until something better came along. She explained that she was teaching a young man to play piano most days. She held the lessons in the living room.

When not doing this, she paid home visits to teach people, she preferred that she said. The Cleaner knew she was embarrassed to live here. It was not what she was accustomed too. She did not work hard all her life to live like this.

Without knowing her story, like the majority of people living in the building, you would think she didn't even work at all. These types are often referred to as Scum by those terrified of walking safely along their own financial tightrope.

The flat was tiny and filled with unpacked boxes. The furniture overly filled each room. Like putting a full-sized sofa in a cubby-hole.

A cat ran past The Cleaner's feet, moving from the living room to the kitchen. That's Satty, the woman said. Calling again, Satty…. The cat ran to her and she picked it up in her arms, snuffling into its head. Who's a good girl? she muffled into her fur. Who's always been here for Mummy? she said.

This woman loves her cat more than other

humans, the Cleaner thought. The cat is The Moon, and this lady may not know it, but she could be a Witch.

The Midwife Pt. 1
The Cleaner passed a car leaking oil in the driveway. It was old and rusted, but whoever had cleaned it had done a great job, he noticed with a smile.

He opened a small gate that led to the porch, bumped his caddy up the step and gently rapped the glass door.

He heard the tinkling of beads and a young lady pulled the door open. She looked tired, he noticed before a word was spoke. Large blue eyes that didn't deserve the sadness they held, looked at him.

I'm The Cleaner, he announced.

She smiled gently. Great, she said pulling the door open, come on in.

She held a beaded curtain back with one arm, which The Cleaner ducked under. They clinked and tinkled as she let them drop, coming to stand by his side.

He surveyed the small two-storey house. It was sparse enough to seem tidy to the untrained eye, but he could tell it hadn't been cleaned since she moved here.

A sharp squawk pierced the atmosphere.

That's Tulip, the lady said, motioning to a branch in the corner of the room where a large white parrot sat.

Hello Tulip, The Cleaner said approaching the cage, how lovely to have a branch instead of a cage. Turning back to the lady he asked, can he talk?

How did you know he was a "he"? She said in shock.

I used to have one myself. You can tell by the heads. The males usually have bigger heads than the females, The Cleaner answered.

Ah I see, the lady replied. No, he can't talk yet. But I'm trying to teach him; any tips?

Talk to him as you would a child, the Cleaner said smiling. Repetition is key. And use the same inflection in your voice every time you speak to him. Invent a voice you only use to speak to him, and one day he'll talk back.

Do you charge extra for the parrot training advice? she laughed.

Not at all Madam, a meal after each days work is all I ask for, he smiled.

Madam! Oh, I've never been called that before, she said placing a hand on her heart. The Cleaner smiled and said nothing.

Let me show you upstairs, she motioned.

The Cleaner watched as she walked before him. She walked on her tiptoes, he noticed. She either suffers from anxiety or has been told to be quiet too often in childhood, he surmised.

What do you do, if I may ask? Asked The Cleaner.

I'm studying to be a midwife at the moment, she replied, If I'm honest with you, I've all the time in the world to clean, but I just really couldn't be bothered. I don't drink or go out any longer. So, I've extra money from my student loan each month, just sitting there. I felt a little bad at first. It seemed lazy...

Not lazy at all Madam. Some people like to clean, others don't. At least you're honest with yourself.

I suppose that's true.

But as you know. I only accept payment in the form of a meal for my cleaning work. So, you'll have to think of a new way to treat yourself with your extra money each month.

You're an angel, she laughed.

The Cleaner smiled.

Crystal Skull Alchemical Collective

Frater OM Emerges
The Man lived with the rainbows before Frater OM came along. He saw only love and light in all. Frater OM brought The Shadow with him, and engulfed The Man in it.

Frater OM was The Magician, and walked a lizard on a leash. Great ferns grew from his legs, deep into Earth. A reward for over throwing the Ulster government, bringing the country to anarchy, then rebuilding it in the vision of Lemuria. He was assisted by the great spirit of Ulster, who was sick of his land being misdealt with. Together they changed a once repressed province, into The New Jerusalem.

And in The New Jerusalem The Man was born.

The Man knew Frater OM before he knew he was Frater OM. He always noticed something in his eyes. A glint of light, along with furry horns. Forked tongue but an incarnation away. Lucifer was not what people were told. He was the great liberator. But did people trust this great guide out of hell?

Frater OM taught The Man how to do magic. With every word he spoke, the knowledge of lifetimes cascaded out like fanning pages of hidden wisdom, from the esoteric womb of The World.

He would help The Man remember, but at the loss of Frater OM's own remembrance. A show of sacrificial bravery. The invisible words between them spoke: I can't do this just now, can you?

Frater Om was The Warrior Of Warriors.

The Work Commences
The Man pondered if any of this craziness was real, then accidentally summoned an angel into his living room one morning, and realised it was.

The connection between Frater OM and The Man, became the point where two over-lapping circles meet. So they named themselves The Church Of The Eye Of God.

Frater OM hated the word God, but The Man convince him to use it during the peak of The Holy Plant Ritual. They were both trapped in the pocket of the Tow-Path Troll and the only way out was to accept the word God into your life. And so Frater OM accepted it and The Man wrote it.

Together they made interdimensional love to Venus while Pan tried to hide his erection in the bushes. They bent each others energetic path-streams into the symbol of infinity, and bi-located simultaneously into different times of each others lives, to watch their younger selves evolve from a different perspective.

Both were initiated into the various etheric esoteric schools of wisdom, and attained the highest order of each. Each time they graduated, they celebrated by taking fist fulls of Uranium Eye Openers and making three-way love to The Mother, FMM. They both ejaculated deep into her soily womb, at the same time, in rib-cracking sobs of pure ecstasy.

Moments like that create an unimaginable bonds between all participants. It was then, they realised their combined magic could open portals to vast dimensions. Portals which they could then go and live in, while the 'human' them continued to live as if nothing was happening.

Somewhere Down The Line
One day The Church Of The Eye Of God had a rift. To be precise, it had developed a rift, but it was on that one day the rift was noticed. Seen, it was like discovering your foot is black, when you thought you may have had an in-growing toenail.

You see, a rival magic circle called The Church Of All Knowing, had been headhunting The Man. They had been watching him since childhood, and appeared at various points of his spiritual evolution to help pass him through onto the next. They were the hidden hand in his life, that had steered him to this point.

One day The Man found himself staring up at a building he had seen in a vision. He had painted a picture of this vision and entitled it 'When You See This Place In Real Life Go In And Tell Them You Saw This Place In A Painting'.

This was prophecy, triple folded back on itself. So The Man went into the building.

It was draped in blue curtains from floor to ceiling. A congregation seated, facing a man in a mobility scooter on a stage, all turned to look at The Man as he walked the aisle.

'You have come', spoke the man in the mobility scooter, from the stage.
'It seems I have', said The Man.
'We have been expecting you', said he, 'For many years'.

'I first saw this place in a vision, so painted a picture of it. I was out walking today and looked up and I'm staring at the same grass banks and white building I saw in that vision, and the picture I painted. Now, my being here seems to be, the final brushstroke in this synchronistic masterpiece'.

'Nice way with words. Although there is no final. But nice to see The Work has paid off', Scooter Man said.

'I thought I recognised you', said The Man through furrowed brows, 'I use to see you all the time in The Old Kingsway. I always tried to catch your eye to say hello, but you never looked at me.'

'It had to be. If we had made eye contact, you would have known too much, too soon'. Scooter Man waved a gammy right hand, 'Come'.

The Man walked up the middle of the seated congregation, their heads turned with each step of his passing.

How very cliched, The Man thought, Do movies inspire life, or life the movies? I suppose these things are like this because it's the way they have to be. There's a pattern to everything. A perfect song. When we second guess ourselves we disharmonize from it.

Scooter Man spoke again:
'We've been watching you since childhood dear one. Your names have always had the vowel E in them. Your eyes have always been blue, and in this story you are known as The Man. We've lived many lives together. Not only me and you. But me, you and everyone in this room. For this is your entire trans-dimensional soul circle. In other words, you are all each others cast in the stories of your individual lives. Like an inter-locking movie that never ends, were each person just swaps costumes with the next. An everlasting dance through the cosmos, back into the mouth of God, which is the vagina. Then experienced from the other side until it folds back in on itself'.

'Wow, You speak very much as I do,' The Man said holding his forefinger to his philtrum, pressing into the indentation, where it seemed to fit perfectly.

'I speak very much like you, for you are The Storyteller of this story, writing these words'.

A Call To Arms
Frater OM sat on a throne of bones. Femurs mostly. He had walked so many lives, the understanding of his past misdoings were collected and transmuted into something for his comfort. But

also something he could break whenever he wanted.

Frater OM was The Knight.
The Man was The King.
This is why it worked.
Check mate.

Then came along Gafarrah The Great.

With that The Church Of The Eye Of God, would start to split into The Right Eye School and The Left Eye School. As the over-lapping circle separated into male/female and became a triangle.

As The Son, returned to The Mother via The Shadow. The Sun, returned to The Earth via The Moon.

With our third member our collective magical powers increased. We really had something with this little scamp of a fella. The Man and Frater OM would confer during meditation sessions:

'Does he know his own power'? Frater OM would hiss-whisper under duel nostril plumes of The Holy Plant.

'Well he's projecting abstract geometry onto my back wall through the bridge of his nose, so I'd say the chances are pretty high', The Man surveyed.

'He's our 'in' into remote viewing, big lad', Frater OM laughed, thumping The Man on the back and a second away from shape shifting into Lucifer himself. Which was what he had incarnated to become. The male aspect of Venus at her highest form.

One night The Man and Gafarrah The Great were out on the town. The Man was high on The Holy Plant and drunk on The Blood Of Christ, Gafarrah The Great was showing him how he could levitate pound coins in the palm of his hands.

Gafarrah The Great had the fire of the lion in his eyes, and knew it. But had forgotten it, but was slowly remembering it. He had a school boy charm and old man laugh. When The Man connected that laugh to the fire in his eye, he remembered their last non-linear life together, as lovers:

They had been in a lesbian relationship from the years 1692 to 1693. Both orphans, they met on the eve of the great summer of summer solstices. He was raven haired and from the fire. The Man was soft and pious and from the earth. Their eyes met and they fell into ultra-dimensional Love. They knew each other on every level of reality all at once, as the bonfires of change burned in the back ground. When they kissed they consumed the gravel and ash of Earth, and cast themselves onto the fire of persecution for the rest of their lives. But they would walk that fire barefooted and brave. Until one day Gafarrah The Great had to leave, and with her last croaking breath she wheezed these words:

'We will meet again in 2003. You will interview me. This will be the beginning of our work together in that life. The cumulation of all this work starts at that moment. Remember me by my eyes and my laugh. See the lion in me that you see in yourself'.

And then he died.

A Sneaky Old Affair
Before Gafarrah The Great, back when it was just the two big lads together, we ruled our world. Frater OM use to run an alchemical brewery. The last beer he ever brewed was imbued with the vaginal and anal juices of Venus, plus his own seamen. They had been having a love affair on the etheric level for a while, and she was convinced enough to collaborate with him on the Earth realm.

Frater OM wanted The World to Know. While Venus wanted The World to Love. So after a long hard chat, they came to a compromise: the world would Know Love.

And so, they donned the alchemical cloaks of old and bathed their hands and feet in saliva. Then Frater OM drew the holy circle of salt, and Venus danced in its middle, and magic was made, good lord, magic was made.

And so, the masses drunk the magic in gargling gulps, and forever did the face of Ulster change. Frater OM was heralded as The New Knight. He ordered utter destruction, until only you existed.

And so, Ulster burned. And with torches ablaze, Frater OM led his army of followers up the steps of

Stormont, locking the doors and burning everyone who had taken refuge inside, alive.

'And it is done'! Frater OM announced to the four elements, offering to them the smoke of the burning bodies. With that, the fifth element of spirit entered his crown like a jack hammer penetrating the heart of Earth herself. All three eyes open, and he saw everything now. He saw that the great spirit of Ulster was his father and they had to fight together to cure the ancestral sickness that he carried.

This was all too dark for The Man.

You see, The Man wasn't as masculine as Frater OM, and would rather file his nails while Frater OM lighted his farts. But this is why it worked. And this is why one day they would plunge a sword into one another's guts, and the next have a lady sew the wounds shut.

Golf Courses
It was Frater OM's idea to turn all golf courses into Temples Of Holy Knowledge. The grounds being mostly used for wandering and contemplation. The ground was The Temple itself, humble and folky. Initiates would sleep on the grass of the old courses at night. Having gotten to a level of ability were they could heat their bodies when needed, without the need of an outside source. This was one of the requirements needed to live at, one of the many, Temples Of Holy Knowledge: Activation Of The Inner Sun.

The Man had developed a technique to unlocked childhood trauma: by walking backwards. You basically walked yourself backwards to various parts of your life that needed looked at with adult eyes, while actually walking backwards on the grass of the golf courses. People laughed at first. Then they tried it and saw Pluto, then Death, then God, then themselves, looking back at themselves.

Everything you've ever been told is wrong. It's all upside down. So start living the wrong way around.

Frater OM refined this technique by combining a breathing pattern to it, along with a visualisation held below the feet. Now not only could he cycle back to points in this life, but all other lives he had lived before the human body had evolved to this point. That meant he could experience life as nature herself, in all her divine expressions, at any stage of her evolution.

It was this development that give him access to The Divine Principle and the ability to bi-locate to any Solar System he wished to visit.

Gafarrah The Great Emerges
The Man and Gafarrah The Great knew each other for over a decade before they *knew* each other. When one remembered the depth of lifetimes they had spent together, it triggered the memories in the other.

And so, they both knew the truth of reality while alive in their current lives.

And so, they done what they've done in every lifetime together: Create a piece of art hidden within the fabric of reality that completely changed the world for future generations, when they saw it.

This is how Gafarrah The Great made it into The Crystal Skull Alchemical Collective:

The Man had a dream Frater OM and he were getting into a car that Gafarrah The Great was driving. On awakening The Man knew someone else was taking the driving seat from now on. A phone call was made, a meeting arranged, and after a little bit of blood loss Gafarrah The Great was sworn into The Collective. Now making it a true triangle, and leading it to it's next stage of development.

At this stage The Collective were looking for premises to work out off. This was the days before the castles. They were still working on themselves, ironing out the last creases of their journey back to The Womb. They rented an old Judo club and started converting it into an esoteric learning centre, then sat back and waited on someone to be brought to them.

One day the door knocked, a lady entered before they could get up to let her in.

'I saw this place in a vision last summer. To make sure I wouldn't forget it I created an art installation about it, entitled 'When You See This Place In Real Life Go In And Tell Them You Made An Art

Installation About It'. While out walking today I happened to look up and recognised the door.'

Frater OM took the lead, shushing The Man back into his seat.

'Yes, we've been expecting you', he lied.

'We?' The Man repeated in his brain. Surveying the empty beer bottles, roach filled ashtrays and half finished 'Church'.

'Oh, hello', said Gafarrah The Great in overalls, emerging with a paint pot and dripping red brush.

The goodness with which he said these words reminded The Man how pure his heart was. He had a truth to him, he was yet to recognize. But when he would, it would change his life forever.

'What's your name?' The Great One asked.

'They call me The Lady,' The Lady said.

So from that moment on, we called her The Lady.

And now our triangle blurred at the edges, threatening to become a square. The Man squirmed. Frater OM oozed glee and Gafarrah The Great started painting the west wall red.

A Break Down
So there we where. Three practising magicians. Just in the process of doing up their first temple space. All on different trajectories of Illumination.

All Illuminating to knowledge-of-self independently and collectively. And a new person shows up.

The Lady was the one who suggested we all have our teeth removed. Anyone who as ever gone through the process of Illuminating will know that the teeth get mighty sore, and the anus itches like a family of fire ants have taken residence there. Months of sleep are lost, and you find yourself understanding pain and discomfort from a whole new angle.

This is just your pranic breathing tube reinstalling from both ends, displaying itself as phantom pain to anyone but the person who is going through it. The act itself may seem extreme, but the group's collective teeth had taken the toll of an Unilluminated lifestyle for many years. They also knew they were getting close to complete telepathic communication, and being able to derive sustenance from The Sun, making food redundant. So why not.

The Lady pulled out her dentures and smiled with nothing but gums. It was quite beautiful in the way a baby with no teeth is beautiful.

'Far less fucking hassle', The Lady gummed, as we squinted to understand her.

She was right. The Man was already searching on his phone for:
How much do a full set of gold dentures cost?

Why not indeed.

A Break Through
One day Frater OM performed a ritual on The
Man that broke him through to the other side.
Unfortunately, the act pushed Frater OM's own
break through to the other side, back a while. He
had made a grand sacrifice for his friend. This
dampened the celebrations afterwards, as The
Man turned to Light before everyone's eyes, and
Frater OM half-sulked in the corner, getting
drunker and drunker.

The ritual Frater OM had devised was surgical, and
called for the torso to be opened up and the
internal organs displayed. The Man had to be put
into a trance for this to work. As he was to be
awake and aware of the full procedure, but in
control of pain and shock levels.

The Man would then be taken on: The Tour Of The
Non-Linear Body -in HD, until he understood the
truth behind each organ and their relation to the
planets. Once realised, he would leave his body
and stay in the astral plane, were the knowledge
was imbued into his energetic memory, to be
carried into his next lives in The Game.

You see, every time you've ever went to the doctors
regarding an aliment. They will check your pulse
and heartbeat. This act of black magic instils a fear
that your pulse and heartbeat will one day be the
death of you. So you try to ignore them, in fear that
if you pay them attention they will stop working.
The quicker you understand that your entire body
wants you to Illuminate, and the doctors want you

dead, the quicker you will die out of their death-reality.

And so The Man died and Frater OM lived.

Conversations With Dog
'This is all I want to do, To sit and talk to you, always.'

'But now you must sit and talk to others. About what we sit and talk about. This is part of your work'.

'What should I tell them?'

'Tell them about how Agents are time travelling to the days of the great mystics, and fooling them. The accounts you have read about ecstatic visions are not always true. Agents of the dark, have been travelling from your time, equipped with products of your day. Stuff so trivial to you, but magical to the people of old.

'An example of this: Two Agents travelled to the time of John Dee. They infiltrate his company by telling him they are Seraphim in human form. Using various cans of deodorant spray, in different scents, concealed up their sleeves. They can produce, what seems to Dr. Dee, magical clouds of enticing fragrances from their hands. With a flick of a concealed lighter, these turn into great flames. This is all done in jest. The entire cosmos is having a laugh, but the people of Earth haven't been let in on the joke. This is how the dark operates. Limiting truth, promoting false.

'Tell them that their society has been brainwashed into thinking sex is wrong. The combining of sex and disease has been planned for a very long time. The pure essence of sex is your lifeline to the divine. But that pure essence has now had malware implanted in it. The malware is fear, shame. guilt and regret. If you feel any of these negative emotions in regards to sex you are sick, and need to fix yourself. Understanding the true nature of sex, will unlock mysteries about the human spirit you never knew existed.

'People have been told they must be a *certain* way sexually. And for the rest of their days they are this one way, and brace with disgust at the thought of being another way. This is the biggest trick. You are meant to be everything, and experience it all. Sex and sexuality are the vehicle for this. You were meant to adapt your sexual preference at various points in your life to learn. This is the risk you take, this is the two fingers up to society. You just feel you shouldn't do this, because you've been told it is wrong for so long. For life is not a straight line, but a series of stories that you must adapt yourself to, to understand the plot. Sexuality is just one of those stories.

'The entire sex of your planet is being transfigured. You will all be A-sexual soon. But to get there you have to experience all the other sexualities, in one lifetime, then be re-born perfect. People who identify as trans-sexual have got it, but have forgotten and think they are in the wrong body.

'Let them know that freckles and beauty spots on the body are maps of star constellations. Detailing each of our individual journeys throughout the cosmos, and showing us where our planet of origin is. That moles and warts are not ugly. Nothing on the human body is ugly, it is all meant to be. Moles and warts are signs of past persecutions, directly related to the advancement of consciousness. Each one you wear, shows how many lifetimes you've been killed because of your beliefs. This is what the image of the witch has been invented for. To help people remember what they were. But the image of the witch has been distorted to one of ugliness. When in truth it is perfect representation of the strive to divinity. Your birth marks are imprints from your previous body.

'All the images you see in your every waking moments have a deeper symbolic meaning. That is what they were invented for, to help you remember what you are. For at a divine level you communicate in symbols, they are the language of the universe. The Virus knows this, so it uses it's own symbols to talk to you, in the form of their corporate logos.

'If you meet someone with no markings at all on them, they have either came to save or destroy you. It is your work to understand this.

'Everything is upside down and around the wrong way. The Virus that has taken over your society is not some monstrous force. It's a 13 year old boy who has learnt some magic tricks. Mostly sleight of hand and the art of distraction. To put it simply: He is pointing his finger and everyone is looking at the finger. He is just distracting you, that's it. Just making you look the other way. He's playing a trick on you, embroiling you in a game he's created.

'All *rights* you fight for are still being fought within the system that created them. You cannot win within this system, it is The Game. You must take yourself out of that system by taking yourself out of The Game, by taking yourself out of the body. Then you win.

'Tell people if they are to learn the power of communication, the *real* power of being able to use their words to design their lives, then they must spend many years talking to themselves. Out loud, not in their heads. For when you speak words aloud the entirety of nature listens, and will help you understand what you need to know. They told you only crazy people talk to themselves, so you wouldn't do it. And you didn't. They told you only crazy people talk to birds, and trees and rivers and clouds so you wouldn't do it. Because once you start talking to these things, they tell you Truth. They are not part of The Game, they see right through it, and want you to see also. They want you to join the party. To know and partake in the great cosmic joke.

'Tell them they have the chance to cure any aliment from a cold to cancer with their breath, whenever they want, if they know how. With one cycle of inhale-pause-exhale-pause, all at the exact same length, you can totally clear the body of all sickness. It is so simple. People have been made to fear their own bodies. That's the real crazy, to think their body is trying to kill them, until one day it does, because they thought it was going to. Everyone is a magician, they're just using their magic the wrong way around.'

The Goat

The Goat lived in the forest, in a small hut beside a larger hut. Inside the larger hut was The Goat's mother. The Goat protected his mother from the people who came through the forest.

Some people who came through the forest were simply lost. The Goat would point them in the direction they should go, to get home. Some people who came through the forest intended on hurting The Goat's mother. He would kill these people. And some people who came through the forest, did so because they wanted The Goat's help.

The Goat was The Guide.

The Goat looked fierce, in the frightening and gay sense of the word. His horns curled high on his head, laced with jewels, on which birds and butterflies sat. His large, wide, blue eyes were unfathomable pools of mesmerism. His large flat nose, plumed smoke signals with The Holy Plant. His teeth capped in gold and studded with diamonds. Long, perfectly styled sideburns, framed his face, while his lengthy goatee elongated it. High-arched brows framed his eyes. His large, pointed ears faced forwards. He blinked sidewards.

He had the torso of a gladiator. Firm muscles under quilted hair, skin scarred from battles and poked with inked stories and symbols. The nails of his hands, long, painted and bejewelled. His legs covered in glistening thick fur. Oiled and perfumed, brushed and tended to. His feet, two shining hoofs, you could see your reflection in. His penis was usually erect with a thick Prince Albert piercing.

The Goat spent his days singing, dancing and drinking with The Forest Nymphs. These were his sisters, who he also made passionate love to. And through that act of lovemaking, they told him best how to be The Guide.

Early one morning the Forest Nymphs woke The Goat from his slumber.

Someone's coming, someone's coming! They chanted in unison. The Goat pried one sleepy eye open and made an assessment on how hungover he was. I'd give this a five out of ten, he thought, not bad for all the wine I drunk last night.

Someone's coming, someone's coming!

Ah of course, that's what woke me, The Goat thought, those chanting Nymphs. Yes, yes, yes. I'm getting up now, he said rising from his bed and opening the door to his hut.

The morning sunshine shot in on beams of gold and white. He felt it on his face and closed his eyes. Just one moment, he said holding a finger up, and basking in the light. Ahhhh, he sighed with the energy of a small orgasm.

Right, why have you woken me, he said to The Forest Nymphs, and why are you not as hungover as I am? The Goat shook his horns, glitter fell all around him and sleeping butterflies awoke and fluttered to the safety of a nearby bush.

What on earth did we get up to last night? He asked everyone and no one in particular.

Someone's coming! Said The Forest Nymphs thrice, this time hiding behind The Goat, peaking their heads out.

OK, shush, he quietened them with a bouncing hand. The silence allowed the sound of the forest to come to life. The Goat's ears piqued as he detected the crunch of leaves under feet. He sniffed the air.

It's a little girl, he said. Smelling the air again, he continued: She isn't lost. She has made her own way here. She hasn't come to harm our mother. She has come for help. Now, help me prepare myself for her!

The Goat and The Forest Nymphs bundled into his hut. He stood in the centre as The Nymphs busied themselves around him. Combing his hair. Painting his nails. Perfuming, oiling, massaging.

You're ready, they said in union.

I am, said The Goat, admiring his reflection in his mirror, I'll see you all in a bit.

With that he left The Forest Nymphs in his hut as he prepared to meet the little girl.

Stepping out into the morning sun, The Goat felt his guts rumble and discretely vomited into a bush. Just how much *did* I drink last night, he pondered, picking the sick out of his freshly set beard.

Whistling and jolly foot fall crunched in the distance. She seems happy, The Goat thought, this should be easy enough.

He walked to a nearby fallen oak, and placed himself upon it, one leg crossed over the other. He took out his harmonica and blew a gentle tune through it. The notes were carried in the morning air, and the birds sang along.

Christ, I need a joint, thought The Goat, I knew I should have had one before this, he admonished himself. But maybe if I had, this hangover would have turned to the nasty side. Best not then.

As he played his harmonica, he went over his lines in his head. The Goat had a series of speeches that he used, depending on the type of person he was dealing with. This was a happy girl, seemingly exploring the woods before the world woke up.

The tone of her whistling placed her in the age bracket of 9-13 years old. A brave girl, to be out this early alone. She's obviously wanting to get away from something, but what could that be?

The Goat pricked his ears up and listened to the

rhythm of her footsteps. They fell like the gentle trot of a pony but were not in time with the whistling that came from her mouth. She was out of sync with something, or someone in her life. Most probably mother or father. It's always the mother or father, The Goat laughed to himself.

He heard her footsteps stop. She must have heard the harmonica and is wondering what the strange sound is. Slowly the footsteps started again, all cautious and inquisitive.

Estimated time of shock and awe, three seconds. 3...2...1...

Oh my god! Came the yelp.

Hello little girl. Don't be afraid. Come and sit with me, The Goat sang-spoke, patting the fallen oak he had placed himself on.

With trepidation the little girl slowly moved toward him.

What are you? She barely spoke under bated breath.

I'm The Goat! And this is my forest. I live just over there, he said jutting a thumb behind him. And your name is?

Dre, the little girl said.

And that is short for? Asked The Goat

Before she could speak, he answered for her: Andrea?

The little girl looked shocked. Noticing, The Goat told her: Oh, that's nothing. Just an ability I have. I can guess the name of anyone who goes by a truncated version of their name.

Well, actually it's Deandreah, said the little girl looking confused, but close enough.

Damn it! Said The Goat slapping his thigh, I used to be so good at that.

He continued: Unfortunately, I was never given the option to have a truncated name, not enough syllables in the original version you see.

Gooooot, he toned, shaping his mouth like an O, to display the one syllable his name held.

You see? My name can only be elongated.
Goaty: I'm not into at all.
Goatse: I was into until the internet ruined it.
Though to be fair I *can* relate. We've all woken up like that in the morning once in a while. Those feisty Nymphs, he said unconsciously rubbing his buttock.
Goatlord: I can live with.

The little girls eyes searched her brow for some meaning in the madness she was hearing.

But just call me The Goat, he finished patting the fallen oak, come and sit with me.

As the little girl approached, The Goat played his harmonica in time with her footsteps. She gazed at him with a mild look of annoyance and stopped walking. He stopped playing. She took a single footstep forward and he blew a note. She stopped and scrunched her brow at him. He stopped playing. He flashed his eyes wide, harmonica still in mouth. Another step. Another note. No steps. Silence. Step. Note. Step. Note.

What on earth are you doing? She said shaking her head in total bemusement.

Playing the song of your journey from there to here, The Goat replied as if she should know this.

I'm a little confused, the little girl said. You must understand how strange all this is for me. My parents have just moved into the area, and I thought I would explore this forest before...

My forest, The Goat interrupted.

...your forest, the little girl continued, before they woke up this morning.

So mummy and daddy are still together, The Goat stated more than asked. And do mummy and daddy ever fight? He asked, adding: Sit, sit, I'll not bite.

As she sat on the fallen oak alongside The Goat, he inhaled her smell. You are of pure light, he said with eyes closed. You must not let anyone take your pure light. I can tell you're a feisty bugger, he wondered if that was the right word to use in the presence of a little girl, but carried on regardless, letting not the hand of Saturn mar the untouched gardens of Earth.

I fucking love that line: he thought, smiling to himself.

The little girl pushed her nose up in puzzlement. He continued:

Dear, what age are you? No, no, no, let me guess. I'm good at this.

He hummed and ahhed, eyes positioned to the upper left of his field of vision. He took at sneaky glance at her chest. She felt it without seeing and raised an arm across her shoulder.

Stupid jacket is far too thick to see if she is sprouting breasts yet, he thought. Then he announced: 13!

12, she interjected straight away. Damn it! The Goat snapped. I'm usually pretty good at guessing ages, he said out loud to no one in particular.

Sooooo….I think I'm going to go, the little girl said, it was….lovely meeting you.

What, we haven't finished yet. No, no I do apologise. Look I was up all night drinking and fucking…whoops. Again, I apologise. That was a swear word.

I know what fucking is, she corrected him.

Course you do, The Goat mumbled, feeling mildly uncomfortable. Continuing: Right, listen. You have come to my forest, the Forest Of The Goat, on this morning, at this time, for a very special reason. You see, only very special people come here, whether they know it or not. And you, my dear, are a very special person. Let me ask you something: Do you like the song of your life?

What?!? The little girl said on the brink of being offended.

Do you like the song of your life! The Goat's voice rose in volume with each word, ending with a slap to his thigh. The change in atmosphere was felt hard. The little girl shrank into herself. The Goat continued: Look, you're a fierce little bitch. But if you don't know how to direct that fire, you're going to burn your house down.

Love that fucking line, The Goat thought again, hope she gets it.

He continued: Look, you come in here, to my forest, whistling and dancing, as happy as Harry. Then you give me this attitude...

Really, I only came here for a walk this morning, the little girl interrupted, my family life is fine. I know what you're trying to imply: Don't let someone take advantage of me if I'm not ready for it. I know when to say no and when to say yes.

Mister Goat, if I may? - Life outside of your forest has expanded in ways I'm not too certain you realise. Little girls like me run the world now. The oppressive male is a long-gone memory, a myth in the annals of time. We don't have to worry about, as you so eloquently put it, but let me put my own spin on it: Saturn fingering us.

The Goat looked surprised then looked dejectedly at the forest floor.

Your job is done, the little girl said patting him on the back, no one wants to destroy Earth any more. No one is coming into your forest to kill your mother. We all love her.

The Goat lifted his head and looked at her smiling face. Really? he questioned. Yes, she answered. But who will I play my harmonica for now? he said. Yourself, I suppose, she answered.

Hmmm, The Goat ruminated sitting up straight, bringing his forefinger to his lips. I suppose I will, he said.

A brief moment of silence befell them.

So… I'll be getting on then, the little girl said rising. I suppose you will, said The Goat. Before I go, she added, why don't you play that harmonica and I'll dance to it.
I would simply love that, The Goat said tears building in his eyes.

And so The Goat blew a tune.

And the little girl danced.
And they both got lost in the beauty of song and
dance.

Well, The Goat spoke after the jollities, It was nice
to meet you Dre.

And you Mister Goat, curtsied Dre.

The Goat attempted a half bow and let out a
thunderous fart in the note of C#.
Did I mention I'd been up all night drinking...

Yes, yes, and fucking, the little girl finished for him,
good for you.

Gluten-Free Girl-Friend

Monday:

Gluten-Free Girl-Friend was writing her book: A Guide To Happiness. The only problem was she didn't know where to start. She had never known happiness. She had pretended to, to the outside world, but inside only sadness. But she thought the writing of this book would bring it.

She sat staring at the textured ivory paper in her vintage typewriter. She had bought both the paper and the typewriter, thinking they would inspire her to write.

What you put in, you get out, she had thought, clicking Purchase, and diving a little further into 3rd Dimensional debt.

Along with the luxury paper and vintage typewriter, she had invested in a stack of self-help books, for aspiring writers. She devoured these for the past seven weeks. Her eyes back-and-forthing behind her glasses, as the steam from her organic green tea steamed up the lens. She forgot the outside world existed.

She had cleared out her spare room and christened it: The Writing Room. She bought a brand-new upcycled writing table, on which the vintage typewriter and ivory paper sat. A high-backed vegan leather chair which cost her more than she wanted to think about, fitted effortlessly under the table. Both sat on top of a distressed bohemian rug, which was on top of newly varnished floorboards, which were distressed to look old.

Everything was positioned to the south facing wall, where the window was. Here she could sit and let the trees in her back garden inspire the words she would write.

On the wall to her left was a floating bookshelf made from reclaimed wood. Filled with the self-help books she had bought, bookended with a statue of Ganesh to the right, and Buddha to the left. Two giants of eastern spirituality holding everything together. To the front of the books, perfectly in the middle was her incense holder. Burning in it tonight was a stick of Enchanted Forest.

And here she was, staring at the textured ivory paper in her vintage typewriter, struck with writer's block, before a word was wrote.

Ah, I know! She exclaimed, The title page.

Thinking typing the title of the book would open the floodgates of inspiration, she carefully clicked out the words:
A GUIDE TO HAPPINESS

A feeling of satisfaction swept over her, with each click of the keys on the vintage typewriter, her book was born.

She rolled out the page and held it close to her

face. Admiring the ink on expensive paper. She held it back further, to see it from afar. The light from the window in her writing room backlit it, and she imagined herself signing copies of the finished hardback, on the night of its launch.

As she turned the paper against the light, she saw a faint watermark within it. She pushed her glasses up and brought the sheet to her face. Inspecting it she deciphered the outline of a mountain range with a crown on top. A line of text curved underneath it: Valley of Moans Paper Mill, it read.

Valley of Moans, she repeated in her head.

She placed the title page face down on the right side of her typewriter. To its left the stack of textured ivory paper was sans a solitary sheet. This made her happy, as she rolled a fresh page into the typewriter, sat back, hovered her fingers above the keys, awaiting the first chapter to come rolling out.

She waited.

And waited.

And waited some more, until her hovering fingers became sore.

She exhaled loudly from her mouth and placed her hands on her lap, as she would when meditating. Maybe if I meditate, I'll know what to write, she thought, Inspiration *is* but only a conscious breath away.

She closed her eyes and felt the air entering and leaving her nostrils. She relaxed her shoulders a little more on each exhalation.

Have you done your homework yet?
Have you finished doing your chores?
If you don't pass these exams you'll never get into university!
I just don't think that boy is right for you!
You're too young to have sex, what if you get pregnant?

Mother.

It was the voice of her mother echoing through her life. She shivered, pushed the past away and opened her eyes. Maybe its not a good time to meditate, she resolved, Maybe I'll look out my window and nature will inspire me.

So she placed her elbows on her writing desk, her face between her hands, and stared out the window.

The coming autumn was stripping the trees of their leaves, and they blew in spare dancing twirls. The late afternoon sun, cast a golden haze through the branches.

She exhaled loudly from her mouth. The incense smoke irritated more than relaxed her. All I want to do is help people, it's my divine purpose to help people. Why can you not help me write this book, she said to the empty room around her.

Tuesday:
Gluten-Free Girl-Friend was sitting in the lotus position, after doing yoga in her living room. She was affirming statements to herself:
May all beings know love.
May all beings know happiness.
May all beings know health.
May all beings be free.

She repeated these lines over and over, under her breath, until she felt they had had an impact on the world around her. Smiling, she opened her eyes and stretched her legs out.

She reached down to her right ankle, with both hands, stretching her lower back. As she massaged her heel, she felt an irritation of the skin. Absently scratching it, it started to smart and sting.

Ouch!

Bending her leg at the knee she brought her ankle close to her face. A flaky patch of skin crept out of her yoga pants, hugging the side of her foot.

She gasped and recoiled in disgust at the mar on her leg. Gingerly inching the leg of her yoga pants up, she saw with horror, that it ran right up her shin. She stroked her finger over the red scaly broken skin, a repellent look creased her face.

She jumped up and pulled off her yoga pants, running to the mirror she had been watching herself in, for a better look. She saw her entire right leg covered in the unsightly rash.

Now it itched like crazy, she dragged her nails
across it, up and down, ahh-ing in equal parts
pleasure and pain. The rash started to weep, then
it started to bleed. She slapped it, feeling the sting
in her heart. The pleasure like the distant echo
from orgasms of old. Then she felt the clock of
shame descend.

Not again, she winced studying the swollen
irritation in the mirror. I thought I was through with
you.

*

As she was applying aloe vera lotion to her leg,
she remembered a time she tried not to think
about. When she was nine years old, and staying
in her Aunt's house for the weekend.
She had awoke from a dream of being trapped in
a house, to find her Uncle standing over her bed,
stroking her leg, inside her nightdress. She
registered the look of shock on his face, when their
eyes met in the dim light of early morning. His
other hand had immediately gone to her face.
Stroking her hair back. There, there. It was only a
dream, he had said. But how did he know, and
why was he there to begin with.

She had never told anyone of this, in the twenty
one years since it happened, in fear of breaking up
the family. Maybe he had just heard me having a
nightmare, and came to comfort me, she tried to
convince herself again.

Scratching at her leg some more, she pushed the memory deep down inside.

I hate men: she affirmed in the silence of herself.

Wednesday:
I can't get rid of this rash, Gluten-Free Girl-Friend barked into her phone as her sister answered.

Well hello to you too, what a greeting. Glad I answered now.

This is serious. My leg is inflamed from my ankle to my knee again. I look disgusting.

Hold on, did you wait until twenty two minutes past two to ring me? Her sister laughed.

No.....she lied.

You did. You're fucking crazy. Just ring me like a normal person, and stop trying to making everything seem like 'divine timing'.

I didn't, it was divine timing, she lied again.

Stop lying to me. I'm your sister. I can tell a mile off. I thought 'Truth' was a pillar in the spiritual community? You're all so big on 'standing in your own truth'.

I didn't lie, she lied a third time.

Whatever. Shouldn't you be done with all that shit by now? So your leg has flared up again. Why don't you go see a doctor?

A doctor, are you crazy?! And let some man I don't know touch my leg? Then get prescribed pills that only mask the problem, and don't heal it?

You're masking the problem by not doing anything about it!

I'm using aloe on it.

Aloe! You've been using aloe on it for the past three years and it hasn't helped.

A lot of help you've been, she snapped.

You phone me up, without saying hello, and unload your shit on me. What the fuck do you want me to do?

I've no one else to talk to. No one ever rings me any more. I never get invited out anywhere. I see everyone tagged in photos of parties I wasn't even invited to.

Get a new group of friends then. You've obviously outgrown them. Maybe ones outside the 'spiritual' community this time? Plus is your 'Goddess Circle' not tomorrow?

That's different. I go *there*. I want people to come *to me*. I fucking hate my life. I do everything in my power to make people happy, and I'm treated like

I don't even exist. I only want to help people you know.

Scratching her pulsing rash she added, I feel so ugly right now.

How can you help people, if you hate your fucking life. Should you not have your shit together before you try to help other people?

I do have my shit together.

Doesn't sound like it.

A lot of help you have been. Goodbye!

As she hung up, she barely heard her sister say: Stop expecting me to be someone I'm not, I'm not just going to tell you what you want to hear......

Thursday:
Now Goddesses, place your hands in The Yoni Mudra, close your eyes, keep your spines aligned, and breathe deep into your sacral chakra: The self-appointed 'Mother' of The Goddess Circle instructed.

Gluten-Free Girl-Friend relaxed, breathed in deep and a small high pitched fart escaped. She clenched her cheeks together and felt the mortification wash over her, as the flatulence echoed around the silent meditation room in the note of F#.

That wasn't me: She said to herself.

Someone coughed behind her to break the tension. Please don't smell, please don't smell, she silently begged her anus.

Now, we call in The Ascended Atlantean Masters, The Appointed Mother continued, ignoring the rising smell of half-digested kale filling the room. Bring your hands to your heart in The Prayer Mudra, take a deep healing breath inwards, and chant The Sacred Atlantean Mantra on the exhalation…

The Appointed Mother of The Goddess Circle intoned the vowel sounds:
A-E-I

The group joined in: A-E-I
Repeating the mantra over and over.

Gluten-Free Girl-Friend felt another fart burble in her lower colon. She clenched her sphincter tight, wishing she had never made that kale smoothie.

Why are you doing this to me, she silently admonished her body. I do everything I can to keep you healthy and you embarrass me like this, in front of my fellow Goddesses.

They're here, they are here, The Appointed Mother wooed. I feel the presence of The Ascended Atlantean Masters. I am a clear channel for them. If anyone has any questions for them, please direct them to me.

Silence befell the room.

When will I find enlightenment? A voice at the back asked.

Dear sister, affirm that you are enlightened, and you will be it, The Appointed Mother said in a slightly different voice.

Thank you, Atlantean Master, the voice at the back replied.

What is my divine purpose? Another voice questioned.

To stand in your power as a conduit of the divine feminine, my dear sister. Hold that space, and spread it to the world, The Appointed Mother replied, her voice just a little wispier than before.

Thank you, Atlantean Master.

The room fell silent again.

The Appointed Mother wooed and swayed like she was in a deep trance.

Gluten-Free Girl-Friend was too disgusted at her own body to ask a question, even though she had prepared a list of them. For the rest of the session she sat in silence, in a huff, berating herself for not having control over her own physicality.

Master, I hate that word, she thought.

Afterwards the members of the circle drank filtered water from copper cups in the kitchen area.

So, would you like to book a space to the India Yoga Retreat next month, The Appointed Mother asked Gluten-Free Girl-Friend.

She didn't but said yes anyway.

Great, if you can send over £1000 within the week, it'll guarantee your space.

Gluten-Free Girl-Friend felt a pang in her stomach as she saw her overdraft become a thousand pounds lighter.

The Appointed Mother stood before her in white linen robes. Her hair wrapped in a tall headdress. Barefoot. She held the gaze of Gluten-Free Girl-Friend's eyes in a wide stare, without blinking, for far longer than was comfortable to look into someone's eyes without blinking.

You look sadder today ,Goddess, opined The Appointed Mother. If you'd like to book a one-on-one healing session with me, we can do it over the weekend? I'm holding very powerful energy at this moment.

Yeah, OK, she agreed, as if she couldn't say no.

Perfecto! Just add £50 to the India Yoga Retreat payment and that'll cover it.

Will do, Gluten-Free Girl-Friend fake smiled, looking anywhere but The Appointed Mother's non-blinking eyes.

Oh, a selected few of us are meeting up tomorrow for food if you'd like to come?

Gluten-Free Girl-Friends stomach turned. Her heart rate increased, and her face flushed.

Mmmmmh? she pretended to ponder.

If you can't, it's fine, The Appointed Mother interjected.

Thank god. She really couldn't. She had somewhere to be tomorrow night.

Yeah, she said, meaning no. I've something on.

No problemo! I'll see you Sunday? Say 11am? For the healing session?

Oh yeah. OK, see you then.

Friday:
Gluten-Free Girl-Friend was sitting heavy in the shoulders, on a plastic chair, one of nine people, sitting similarly in a circle of plastic chairs. Her back ached and the only way to ease it was to sit slumped.

How have I got a sore back, when I'm a qualified yoga instructor? She chastened her spine. I must look a sight sitting here all bent over.

Someone cleared their throat before speaking: For the new members, let's take turns introducing ourselves, and telling the group a little about why we are here. We'll start with me then move to the left.

That meant it was Gluten-Free Girl-Friend was last to talk. So, she started planning out her story in her head.

Blocking out the other voices, her eyes darting back and forth, behind her glasses, as she wove the memories into narrative.

Time froze in an internal mosaic of her recent past, while voices played tag around her.

She heard someone clear their throat and looked up at the group, all eyes were on her, signalling her turn.

She composed herself and sat up a little straighter. Swallowing hard she began: My name is...is...

Compose yourself, she commanded silently.

Clearing her throat, she began again:

My name is...Uhhhaahh. She broke down in tears. A hand to her right gently patted her shoulder. She gasped in little inhalations.

Comforting words came: It's OK, go on if you can.

Taking a deep breath in, she wiped her nose with the sleeve of her cardigan, and raised her head, but kept her eyes on the floor. Stretching her eyes wide under her glasses, she blew a long exhalation out of her mouth.

Forgetting to tell the group her name, she went right into her story:

I was part of a Buddhist Death Cult.

The other members of The Cult Survivor group nodded solemnly, a few faint gasps faded into silence.

She continued, stifling tears:
I went to one of their meditation retreats. It was lovely, everyone was friendly and I felt accepted for the first time in my life. After the retreat I started going to their weekly meetings, where I eventually volunteered. I would hand out flyers in the street, offering passers-by freedom from their suffering.

The deal was when I got enough people to come, I could apply to become a teacher. A teacher would lead the meditation classes, and I've always saw myself as a teacher, so I jumped at the chance.

One day while I was cleaning up after a session, I was offered a teaching position. They said I showed so much promise, I didn't need to apply. They said the light in me was so pure, they would 'fast-track' me.

I was brought into the inner sanctum. A room only teachers were allowed in. Here a large picture of an old man adorned the wall, above a table covered in flowers and offerings. They told me this was Master. It was his word they were spreading.

At first I was confused as I had thought it was the word of Buddha himself we were spreading. But they told me Master's interpretation of Buddha's words were more suited to a western mindset.

Master's interpretations were compiled in a book, simply known as The Book, from which they taught from. I was told to study it each day for nine hours, with an hour of the meditation before, during and after. I was not to have sex or masturbate. A strict vegan diet was given to me, and my head was shaved.

I was to adhere to this for nine months. Only then would I 'get my robes'. Getting the robes meant you were now a teacher. And now I was told: You must give your life over to these teachings.

I agreed, all I wanted to do in life was teach others. But I didn't realize what they really meant when they told me that.

On the night I got my robes, a party was thrown for me. I stood looking at myself in the toilet mirror of The Centre, swaddled in burgundy and yellow. My head shaved and my face free from make-up.

I've done it, I thought, I'm where I've always wanted to be. I'm a teacher.

There was a knock on the toilet door. Just a minute, I called. I smiled at my own reflection for the first time in years, then turned to open the door.

A young volunteer fell in, giggling to himself. He had only started a few weeks ago. As handsome as he was eager to learn the teachings. I could smell alcohol on his breath in the close proximity.

Have you been drinking, you can't drink in here, I told him.
Ssshhh, he laughed playfully, producing a hip flask, popping it open and holding it up.

To you! He toasted. On this special night, may you be blessed into non-suffering for the rest of your incarnation.

I laughed at how much he'd picked up in a few short weeks. He took a slug and offered it to me. I refused, I've got my robes, I can't consume alcohol any longer, I said.

Come on, it's your last chance before a life of nunnery beckons.

I laughed, he was so innocent and charming. The smell of alcohol and our closeness in the small toilet, ignited a feeling I had not felt in nine months: How fun it was to do something you're not meant to.

But I composed myself. Being a teacher meant more to me than having fun now. Helping others was more important than indulging myself.

These robes are everything to me, I told him.
OK, he nodded agreeably.
He stretched his arms out for a hug, I laughed,
then we embraced.

As we did, I could feel he had a slight erection
bulging in his jeans. It wasn't intimidating. It felt
nice. It was the first time someone had been
aroused by my energy in ages, and I felt myself
start to become turned on.

We pulled away, for a split second I was about to
unlock the door and walk out of there. But as our
eyes met, something sparkled between us, and I
pulled him in and started kissing him.

I unbuckled his belt and let him do the rest. I hiked
up my robes and sat on the sink, opening my legs
and pulling my burgundy pants to one side.

He kicked off his jeans and underwear, I pulled
him to me, my arm hooked around his neck. I
guided his erection inside of me, and we made
love in the toilets of The Centre.

I told him not to cum inside me. After I had
orgasmed, he pulled out and ejaculated over my
new robes, by accident. He was apologetic,
running the water and pawing me clean. But by
this point I was already numb with shame.

Go, just go. I scolded him as I fixed myself in the
mirror. The same mirror where, five minutes ago, a
Buddhist teacher had looked back at me. Now, a
broken little girl, dressed up as a Buddhist teacher

looked back at me, with a large cum stain on her robes.

We never spoke of it again, and he eventually stop volunteering a few weeks later. In that time, I was moved into The Sangah, a little down the road from The Centre.

The Sangah was a complex where all the teachers lived. I gave up my flat and everything connected to my old life to be there. I lived rent free, my food and everything I needed was supplied to me. All my links to the outside world were completely severed.

I taught at The Centre, giving meditations, and leading retreats at our various Centres across the country. I was happy, but the memory of that night in the toilets never truly left me.

One day I was summoned to the main office of The Sangah. A line of seven teachers sat at one side of a table and motioned for me to sit on a small wooden chair opposite them.

A discrepancy has been brought to our attention, the teacher sitting in the middle said, smiling in a way that didn't go with the words he spoke. I looked to the faces of my fellow teachers. They smiled at me. But behind the smiles were looks of judgement I hadn't felt since I was in school.

I had always known this day would come. Deep down inside I knew it would come out eventually. Word had gotten back to them of what had happened in the toilet that night. I had no idea how. But I knew this was it.

We will say nothing more of it now. But we want you to go to your room and study The Book. Specifically, the chapters on The Hell Realms.

Sick rose in my stomach. I knew what they alluded to. The Hell Realms are where you go, if you have 'Got your robes', and break The Vows. They are what await you after this life. How far down into The Hell Realm you will go, and for how long you stay, depends on the severity of The Vows broken.

Your food will be brought to you, but rationed, he continued still smiling. And you must stay in your room until you are told to rejoin us. We will bring you a bed pan and jug to relieve yourself each morning, and we will replace them with fresh ones the next day.

I was in that room for three months, eating one small meal a day, before I was allowed to rejoin the group and start teaching again. Shitting into a bedpan and pissing into a jug, which if I needed to go in the morning, would stink the room out all day and night long, until they changed them the next morning. Literally shitting where I ate, and slept, and lived.

I had made my peace that I would live my next life in The Hell Realm, until my sins had been annulled. It terrified me, but it made me commit even harder to truly teaching the words of Master. I thought the harder I taught, the less horrific The Hell Realm would be.

By the time I was allowed to rejoin the group, a flock of newly ordained teachers had moved into The Sangah. I was told my first task was to give The Presentation.

The Presentation was a guided introduction to The Sangah. We used a video package on a large flat-screen television, that was wheeled into The Meditation Room on these days. I was to simply talk the newly ordained through it. Like giving a power-point presentation.

I was so happy to be accepted back and teaching again.

As everyone gathered in The Meditation Room, I prepared in the adjoining tea-room. Once they were seated and comfortable, I entered. They all stood and bowed at my arrival. I nodded solemnly, walking to the small stage and sat on the cushion. As I sat, everyone sat.

I guided them in a small meditation before starting the video package. It was such an honour to be in this position.

As the video played, I talked them through it. Giving them details to go with the images. The faces all looking back from me to screen, with intent concentration. Nodding and smiling along.

Half-way through, the video cut out, and grainy black and white footage took its place. I was confused and looked to the other teachers standing at the back for help. They just smiled back at me, two of them diverting their gaze to their feet.

I turned to the screen and saw it was CCTV footage, shot from high, of two people having sex. My heart thundered a blast-beat in my throat as I realized it was from inside the toilet of The Centre. From the night when I got my robes.

Gasps filled the room, as the flickering video showed me sat upon the sink, robes hiked around my waist, having sex with the volunteer. I turned my face from it and closed my eyes. Tears building and my cheeks inflaming, I felt sick with an embarrassment I hadn't felt since childhood.

I openly started to weep. I heard the television click off and the room fall silent.

Footsteps approached me, then a hand on my shoulder. I glanced up through the tears, to see one of the teachers looking down at me, smiling. I closed my eyes again and wept as he started to speak.

His words were lost in the whirling noise of my mind, but I knew he was warning the new group: That this right here, would be the consequences for breaking The Vows. This is how committed we are to the Masters words.

He was rubbing my shoulder, consoling me, as he spoke. The image of his smiling face burning a hole in my brain.

I wanted to run to my room, pack my bags and leave. But my body was glued to the spot. Even if I did run I had nowhere to go. I had given up everything to be a teacher.

That night he came to my room. I was huddled on my bed with my sheets wrapped around me, damp with tears. I was told: He was sorry that had to happen, but it was just the way things are done around here.

All day I had been planning my escape. It wasn't that I was imprisoned there. It was that once I left, I had nothing. No home, no money. I had cut all ties to my friends and family when I joined The Sangah.

I was told I would be getting sent to help build a new temple in Sierra Leone. A white girl dressed as Buddhist in the middle of a war zone, I wouldn't last a week.

The next morning I packed my bags and sat on my bed awaiting the knock on the door. I looked down at my burgundy robed body and had never felt as stupid in my life.

The knock came and I was escorted down to the waiting car. These people I thought of as my family, discarding me so easily, while smiling the entire time, like it was normal to behave like this.

As I was led out the doors, I saw a large black SUV waiting on the road. My two escorts left my side, the doors of The Sangah gently closed behind me, as the sounds of normal life filled my ears for the first time in forever.

A passing car beeped, startling me, I looked to see a group of lads pointing and laughing out the window at me. What must I look like? I sad-thought.

A large man in a black leather jacket got out of the passenger door of the SUV and slid the side door open. I looked in and saw the sandalled feet under burgundy robes, of two others. The man reached out for my hand to guide me in.

As I walked towards the open door, I handed my bag to him. I looked inside the SUV and caught the terrified glances of the people in the back. I looked to the man's face and he was smiling. I was so sick of people smiling smiles that didn't mean what they conveyed.

The man placed his hand on my shoulder and started to gently push me into the back. My heart beat so hard it flashed bright white in my eyes.

Help!!! I screamed. The man, startled, stepped back on one foot. Help!!! I yelled again. He grabbed at my robes. We struggled as he tried to bundle me in. I felt a strength within myself I didn't know was there. I pushed him in the stomach, creating separation. He grasped a fist full of my robes, but I snaked out of them, my saddles coming off in the fray. In nothing but my burgundy pants (we weren't allowed bras) I ran into the moving traffic without looking.

 Help!!! I screamed as cars zoomed by on either side. But no one stopped. They just aggressively honked their horns at me.

I ran to the pavement at the other side and into a park, holding an arm over my exposed breasts, my bare feet aching, I didn't stop running until I saw a man in a wide brimmed hat walking a Dobermann.

Help me please. Someone's chasing me: I begged him. He stepped back and looked at me in shock, trying to compute what was happening.

I looked at the entrance to the park, and the man from the SUV had just begun to come toward us.

Please help. It's him, I screamed, that man. He's after me.

The man dropped his dog lead and walked towards him.
Hey you! He shouted, his walk turning into a sprint, as he give chase.

The man from the SUV turned and ran back to it, slamming the door shut and speeding away.

I collapsed on the gravel path crying, nothing seemed real. It was like a nightmare.

Lying there with my head in my arms, a sniffing wet nose poked through the gap in my elbow. The man's dog was lapping at my face, as if to wipe away my tears.

I put my arm around it, as its dark brindle hair and whiskers tickled my naked skin. I laughed for the first time in months, as the dog huddled in-between my arms. I felt more love from this dog than from anyone in the time I'd been at The Sangah.

Snaps of gravel grew louder, as the man in the wide brimmed hat ran back to me. I looked up at him, he was holding his knees, trying to get his breath back. His hat on the ground beside him, his hair dripping with sweat.

Let's get you home love, he said regaining his breath.

*

In the following months, my sister let me stay with her. I didn't leave the bedroom for weeks, searching the internet for details about The Sangah.

I found pages of survivor groups related to them. People sharing stories just like mine. Warning others about them. I felt so stupid.

After contacting an admin of one of these pages, I was told of the real outcome of those sent to build temples in other countries.

Saturday:
Gluten-Free Girl-Friend awoke from a dream with a bang. Her heart raced as she integrated from the world of sleep to the world of wake. She sat up in bed and looked at her clock. It had just gone three fifteen in the morning.

Bang!
The noise startled her, and her heart jumped to her throat.

Bang! Bang!

It was coming from her writing room. She waited, holding her breath, waiting for it to come again.

It didn't.

Climbing out of bed, she turned on the lights, and listened. She made her way into the hall and turned on those lights too.

The door to The Writing Room was ajar, and she peered at the darkness it held, sliding in a hand, she searched for the light switch.

Clicking it on, the room illuminated in an orange glow. Her ivory paper was slung across the floor, as the curtains billowed in the wind coming through the window.

Awww, the window, she exhaled with relief. The fucking window, she laughed walking towards it, closing it against heavy gusts that pulled back.

As it shut, the room fell silent. The noise of the outside night cut off. She looked at the papers that had blown across the floor. Clean, pristine, ivory sheets, fanned out in casual disarray.

She squatted and started gathering them in a neat pile. The residual smell of incense still in the air from last night, when she had come in here to work, but was uninspired.

Levelling the sides of the paper together, a sheet in the middle refused to yield. She separated the block and saw it was creased. Holding it up to the light to smooth it out, she saw the watermark again.

Valley of Moans Paper Mill, she read out loud. Running her thumb over the logo of the crowned mountain: Valley of Moans.

Leaving the block of straightened paper beside the typewriter, she went back to her bedroom and turned on her phone. Half hoping to hear the ding of messages that had been sent to her as she slept, but no dings came.

Bringing up the search engine, she typed: Valley Of Moans and pressed the looking glass icon. A series of links directed her to sites describing a mountain range. She clicked on the images icon and scrolled through pictures of rocky outcrops, stone walls and birds eye views of tiny towns, below sky reaching peaks. An image of a beautiful lake caught her eye: The Sleeping River, read the title.

She hit the maps icon and entered her postcode to see how far she was from this place. 42 miles. It would take just over an hour to get there. She looked over to her clock and it was nearly three thirty-three.

Divine timing! I must *have to* go to this place, she thought.

She swiped her hand over her phone to take a screenshot of the directions and lay back in bed. What am I going to do when I get there, she wondered. She remembered the wind that had blown her window open and awoken her. She shivered a little at the thought of being outdoors in it.

But the time *was* three thirty-three, at the exact moment I was looking at the directions. If that's not a sign...

She picked up her phone again and searched for camping equipment with next day delivery. If she bought everything she needed now, she would *have* to go. She would leave it up to the universe to decide what time she left. Once that delivery driver knocked her door, she would unpack everything from the boxes, and load them into her car. That would be her sign that it was time to go. Time froze as she read the reviews and compared prices to all of her purchases.

Done.

Excitement danced in her stomach, and she let out a little squeal at the thought of adventure. Looking at her clock she saw it was five minutes past five and let out a bigger yelp of excitement.

She fell back laughing. Wow, she said out loud, looks like I'm going camping in The Valley of Moans.

Sunday:
Gluten-Free Girl-Friend sat waiting on her delivery to come. She had spent the morning emptying her cupboards of any food she could bring to cook on the camping stove she had bought, along with:

A high performance two-person tent.
A water-repellent natural duck down sleeping bag.
An inflatable mattress with hand pump.
An 8.1watt LED camping lantern.
A fleece, waterproof jacket, trousers, hiking boots and hat with attached mosquito net.
A cooking mess set with two tins, a fork, knife and spoon.
A compass.
A collapsible 8 litre water carrier.
A 70-litre large capacity mountaineering backpack.

She had planned to camp until Tuesday, that would give her two nights there. Avoiding the mass of weekend campers, she hoped to have the place to herself, so she could work on her book amidst the beauty of nature.

While awaiting the knock of the delivery driver, she began to meditate.

She was just reaching a deep stillness when her phone beeped. Bringing herself out, she saw a message telling her: Your delivery is three stops away.

Yes! She air-punched.

Checking the clock, it was a little after one pm.

She ran things over in her mind:
If the delivery comes within the next half an hour, I can load up and be out of here by two. With Sunday traffic I should make it there by three. Park, unload, suit up. The hike there takes three hours. Three, four, five, six, give or take half an hour. I should be set up and eating supper around the campfire for around seven thirty.

The door knocked.

Yes! She air-punched again.

*

She arrived at the car park for the mountain range at four thirty, an hour and a half longer than she thought. Stupid GPS, had been her mantra on the journey there, leading her down unknown country lanes that went nowhere.

She changed out of her clothes and put on her fleece, waterproofs, hat and hiking boots. She filled her backpack with her supplies, strapping in the rolled sleeping mat to the bottom, and the rolled up sleeping bag to the top. She filled the water carrier from bottles of water she had brought and hooked it to the side of the bag. She picked it up to test its weight, and nearly pulled a muscle in her arm.

Ouch, she said shaking away the pain. She hadn't expected it to be that heavy. Hopefully carrying it on her back would counteract the weight. She also had her tent to carry, leaving one free hand to hold the directions to The Sleeping River, in the heart of The Valley of Moans.

It was coming up to four minutes past five when she started out on the hike. The backpack was heavy but she was sure she could carry it for the three hours it took to get there, stopping once in a while to rest.

Within minutes of walking from the car, rain started to spit. Then in a blink it came down in walls. She pushed her shoulders to her ears, turning to look at her car in the distance. The rain came down even heavier, and for a second she considered giving up and going back.

Fuck it, just do this, she affirmed to herself.

*

The ground grew soft and muddy as she trundled on. Her steps becoming shorter as the new hiking boots dug at her heels. She took out her phone to check how far along she was. She had been walking for what felt like a good hour and was still miles from the camping spot.

Her back ached as she threw off the backpack to rest. Sitting on it she removed her boots, flaps of moist broken skin exposed her red raw heels underneath, weeping and bloody.

She placed her bare feet in the wet grass. The dampness stinging, then soothing them. The rain had given up, but she was soaking with sweat. She removed her fleece and threw it into a thick bushel of wild grass. Sorry mother nature, she apologised to the earth for littering.

She took a swig of water, letting it run down her chest, and dumped the rest over her head. She had never felt so dehydrated in her life. It was starting to get dark, and she vowed to make it to there before it was pitch. She stood up, hooked her arms into the backpack and started out again.

*

It was nine thirty when she had to stall and rest. She had walked for three hours, only stopping to relieve her bulging backpack of items, too heavy to carry.

At one stop she left her camping stove, which was the heaviest thing there, and the majority of tinned food. At the next stop her lantern. After that her inflatable mattress and hand pump.

Fuck it, I'll sleep on the ground in my sleeping bag, as long as I get there.

She had taken off her boots, tied the laces together, and hung them from the strap of her backpack. Barefoot was better than the agony of breaking in new boots. Her waterproof trousers had been rolled to her knees. Her jacket had been stuffed into the backpack along with her t-shirt. Her sports-bra the only remaining clothing on top. At this point she didn't care who saw her and what they thought, she just wanted to get to where she was meant to be.

She breathed slow and deep, every breath feeling like it could be the last one before she passed out. She had no water until she got to The Sleeping River.

Three hours! Three fucking hours! She shouted into the silence of oncoming night.

Three hours, if I didn't bring all of this shit. She stood and kicked her backpack, forgetting she was barefoot. Fffffuuuuu... she gritted through her teeth, rubbing her toes, hopping on one leg.

FUCK! She screamed skywards.
Planting her face in her hands, she started to laugh at the absurdity of it all. I am fucking doing this no matter what, she said bending to shoulder her pack, even if it kills me.

*

She arrived in The Valley of Moans just after eleven that night. The light of her phone and the moon were the only illumination she had in those moments. She couldn't believe she had made it. If it wasn't for the full moon reflecting The Sleeping River, she would have never navigated there.

She collapsed face first in a clearing of soft grass without even taking her backpack off. She started to cry with relief, smelling the earth in her face as she did. Rolling over she looked at the full moon, laughing maniacally, it looked like the face of a baby seal, she thought.

With barely enough energy left, she wriggled out off the backpack and stumbled towards the water. Dropping to her knees she drank it in spilling gulps from her cupped hands.

She looked back at her pile of stuff, greatly decreased from when she had started out. No way I'm putting that fucking tent up tonight, she vowed.

Pulling the sleeping bag from the backpack, she lay it on the ground, climbed in and zipped it up.

This'll do, she whispered closing her eyes, This is perfect.

She spoke to the sleeping bag as she drifted off into a deep dreamless sleep: You're a sarcophagus of hot comfort.

Monday:
Gluten-Free Girl-Friend awoke to the heat of the rising sun on her face. Without opening her eyes, she just felt it upon her skin. For a second she had thought it was the sun coming in through her

bedroom window, until she remembered she was miles from anywhere, in a sleeping bag on the ground.

She pulled herself up and looked at her scattered belongings. They sat where she had left them. She turned and for the first time saw The Valley of Moans and The Sleeping River in all their dazzling glory. The morning haze made it look like a dream.

Wow, she mouthed. Using that word with as much honesty as she could ever recall.

A feeling of accomplishment filled her heart. She had done it. She had done what she set out to do. Putting on her glasses, she looked around the valley. On the other side of The Sleeping River was the distant figure of a man. He seemed to be packing his stuff up, getting ready to leave.

She was both happy and sad. Sad that she could have had someone close by, but happy that she was now alone.

The immense space she was situated in gave her a profound sense of freedom she had never felt before. She climbed out of her sleeping bag, stripped naked and walked down to The Sleeping River.

It was ice cold as she tip-toed into it, her feet sinking into the soft mud. She scooped up handfuls of water, scooting it into her mouth. She walked farther out until the water came up to her waist, then sat down submerging herself in it.

The sounds of the morning ceased as she held herself in the cold darkness underwater, breaking back through with a revitalised gasp. She stood and walked back to the shore, shivering and rubbing her arms as the water level made its way down to her ankles.

*

After she had erected the tent, in a battle of womanhood versus camping engineering, she emptied her backpack. The majority of the food she had brought had been left on the hike, to lighten the load.

She now had in her possession:
One tin of soup. No can-opener to open it.
A packet of crushed instant noodles. No camping stove to heat them.
A compass. That she didn't know how to use.
A cooking mess set. That was useless without food.
Her waterproofs and t-shirt. Moulded into a damp misshapen ball.
Her hiking boots. Like new, but stained with blood around the inner heels, and at this moment, the personification of evil.

Her stomach rumbled. She hadn't eaten since before leaving yesterday afternoon. Then it groaned louder, and she felt it turn and swell. A sharp pain drew her hands to it.

She felt herself become light headed, as a quickening pressure built up in her guts, and a feeling of dread rose within her. Oh god, she exclaimed, is that water even drinkable?!

She half ran to a near-by bush, squatted and emptied her colon of hot diarrhoea. It came out like high pressured brown water from a faucet in an old house.

She squat-danced, manoeuvring her feet so not to shit on them. Relief slowly came with each burst of loose stool.

*

Her phone finally died just after mid-day, not that there was any signal out in the wilds but it was her last connection to the world. I need to eat something or I'm going to be a miserable bitch until I leave tomorrow, she thought, lying in her tent naked, enjoying the safe seclusion it brought.

Using her teeth, she ripped her waterproof trousers into frayed shorts, and slipped them on. She pulled her sports bra off and ripped it into strands. Tying the shorn-off legs of the trousers around her feet, she fastened them with remnants of her bra, making makeshift shoes, cursing the hiking boots to holy hell. She placed her glasses on, pushing them up her nose. Finally, she put on her hat and pulled the mosquito net down round her face.

Stepping out of the tent she felt like a warrior in a strange world, empowered in the heart of nature. A bad-ass motherfucking bitch, with her tits out. She squatted and stuck her fingers in the dark mud. Pulling them out, she raised the mosquito net and drew two thick lines under her eyes.

Delving her fingers back into the mud, she retracted them out and drew a large crescent moon on her stomach, and a blazing sun on her chest, the rays covering her nipples. Come at me day, she barked, come at me.

*

After walking around the perimeter of The Sleeping River, she came to a bush with berries and after inspection picked some. Walking more she found an old tree stump with mushrooms growing out of it, and after inspecting them, picked some. Lastly she walked through a patch of dandelions, snatching a handful up.

She was well aware of the dangers of poisonous plants. But having used herbal medicine for so long she was pretty confident these couldn't hurt her.

She found a large stick, which she carried like a staff. Singing at the top of her voice as she walked, listening to it echo throughout the valley. Popping berries into her mouth, she flapped her arms like the birds that sung around her. Ripping the heads of the dandelions and chewing them like a cow. The mushrooms, upon mastication, immediately released a flood of foul liquid that shook the gag reflex into action. She swallowed this regardless, sure of its nutrient value and ground through the remaining other-worldly mush.

*

The afternoon had settled in by the time she got back to her tent. Exhausted she zipped up the door, lay on top of her sleeping bag and closed her eyes. Strange geometric shapes melded together behind her lids. She snapped them back open and stared hard at the roof of the tent. Closing them again, her heart started to beat faster, a heavy drowsiness swept over her, and the geometric patterns became more vivid.

She pried her eyes open, like it was the last thing they wanted to do. Inside the tent was filling with a deep pulsating design. A design made from many circles overlapping each other. She looked down at her hands and her skin breathed and swirled before her eyes.

You have got to be fucking kidding me, she whispered, as anxiety engulfed her. I checked those mushrooms, they were normal edible mushrooms, I checked them…shit, how many did I eat?

She couldn't keep her eyes open but didn't want to close them. She tried not to think about being in the middle of nowhere, by herself, about to trip out on magic mushrooms.

Stay calm. Stay calm. Stay calm. She panted. Don't bring fear into the trip, don't bring fear into the trip.

All she could do now was close her eyes, lie back
and hope it went well.

*

Time had stop existing long ago as she watched a
giant spider climb a sparkling web made out of
crystal raindrops. Its abdomen swaying like it was
twerking in slow motion. It was too beautiful to be
as terrifying as it should be. Crystal silk spun out of
its spinneret as its rear legs weaved it into the most
perfect structure she had ever seen.

You are standing at the edge of consciousness,
looking out into infinity: A voice told her. As she
seemed to be standing at the edge of
consciousness, looking out into infinity. Looking out
into timelessness. Looking out into herself.

We just go on for forever, she thought.

Like a cut scene in a movie, she was now gazing
up at a Dobermann sitting in the lotus position, a
planet rotated between its legs. It seemed like the
largest thing she had ever seen. People call me
Pluto but call me whatever you like. Some people
call me The Boatman, the Dobermann said to her,
I'm the end of level boss in the game of life. I'm
the one who guides you back home.

She was frozen in the magnitude of it all. The awe-
inspiring gorgeousness of it all. She moved her
fingers as much as she could. Stroking the base of
her tent, it felt like nothing she had felt before. It
felt like it contained a story all of its own.

She gently opened her left eye, gazing down at her feet. The inside of the tent was alive with flowering light. A light not distant from her body, but *coming* from her body, relative to it. She and the light around her were as one.

She moved her big toe and watched in fascination at every muscle that worked to make that movement possible. My body is so beautiful, she thought for the first time ever.

Closing her eyes again, the darkness swallowed her. She heard a distance drumming and chanting:

Duh, duh duh, duh duh.
Duh, duh duh, duh duh.
Duh, duh duh, duh duh.
Duh, duh duh, duh duh.

She watched herself walking deep beneath the earth, totally naked.

Duh, duh duh, duh duh.
Duh, duh duh, duh duh.
Duh, duh duh, duh duh.
Duh, duh duh, duh duh.

The drumming and chanting grew louder. She emerged into an underground world and watched a large circle of women dancing around fire, that licked high into the darkness above them. The chanting and drumming were coming from them.

As she walked closer, she could make out the mantra they rhythmically sang:

AH – BABA – BARA.
AH – BABA – BARA.
AH – BABA – BARA.
AH – BABA – BARU.

The circle opened up as she got closer and she saw a woman sitting amid the flames, impervious to them, basking in them. The woman raised a finger and beckoned her to come closer.

As she did the circle closed and the lady in the flames stood and walked out of the fire towards her. She seemed to embody all the elements that made up Earth, in human form. She was Earth in human form. *She* was Earth in human form.

A frayed black shawl swung to the beat of the drums as she walked with her head bowed.

Coming toe to toe, she lifted the shawl from her head allowing her eyes to be seen. They glowed luminous blue light. She spoke telepathically:

The book you're writing. Write it without words. You cannot tell people anything. But you can show them.

Do not let people talk and treat you the way they do. You are a very important person on Earth at this moment. You may not know what you are, but I do. And anyone who wrongs you in actions or words, will suffer the consequences.

There are people on Earth fulfilling a mission, most of them don't know this, but whoever wrongs that person on the mission, will pay. Whoever helps that person on the mission, will be rewarded. One thing to remember when speaking to a person on a mission: Hold your tongue, lest your words bring your world down.

A person on a mission has no control over this. They are protected by a higher power. And that higher power cares not for those who make life harder for the person on a mission. The person on a mission's life is usually hard enough.

You are one of these people on a mission.

All of your spiritual practises are useless. Forget them. Just live a normal, contented life, and all will come. You are already everything you need to be. Get drunk. Smoke cigarettes. Dance to loud music. Fuck as many men as you want.

Gluten-Free Girl-Friend spoke telepathically for the first time:

Uh, I hate men.

Without man you wouldn't be here. Why do you hate men?

I've had nothing but bad experiences with them.

Since when?

All my life.

When was the first time you had a bad experience with men?

From my first boyfriend when I was 16.

No, before your first boyfriend.

I didn't have a boyfriend until I was 16.

But something happened to you, that made you resent men before you ever got into relationships with them.

I think I was raped when I was 9 by my uncle.

And have you forgiven him for it.

No! I hate him for doing it. He ruined me.

Well then, those feelings you have for your uncle will represent themselves in every relationship you'll ever have, until you forgive him. He'll rape you over and over again through every male who enters your life, until you forgive him.

How can I forgive the person who raped me?!

He raped you, for you to one day have the strength to forgive him, not in person, but in your heart. Can you not see the act of forgiveness is above the act of rape?

But why did it have to happen in the first place?

For you to truly understand the power of forgiveness. It's what you came here to learn. How to forgive.

*

Ababbara brought her mouth to Gluten-Free Girl-Friend's nose and breathed new life into her nostrils. She would never breathe the same way again.

Tuesday:
Gluten-Free Girl-Friend awoke.
Gluten-Free.

Esmeralda

Esmeralda was hiding in her attic. The smell of old and dust and rank exclusion filled her nose, but she dared not sneeze. The crunching grumble of concrete and syncopated foot fall approached from the north.

The snap of gunfire echoed above the monstrous chorus of heavy rolling artillery and marching jackboots.

She had visions of her friends and neighbours, those who were still alive, being picked off by marksmen. The aggressors stomped through the desolation of their particular vision of preformed war.

Esmeralda remembered this once living street full of commerce and laughter and community. Now grey rubble and dead bodies filled it.

*

The Artist was in his living room, working on a 9'x9' canvas painting. He stood barefoot on the white sheet he laid out before commencing each piece, a glass of high caffeine wine in one hand, a fat joint burning the fingers of the other. Wagner blasted from two speakers sat atop high-chairs either side of the canvas at the south facing wall.

During The Outbreak, The Artist reclaimed art as the true purveyor of truth in the world known as reality. He was heralded a hero, while the masses coughed and wheezed.

He was The Great Revealer, a magician who pulled the veil from the collective eyes of mankind. He was kind. He was man. He was The Kind Man

He thought to himself: As children we created a world to live in with our creative imagination, and we were supported to do so. Then we were cast out into the wilderness of the world as teenagers, to find our way home again. Most people are still stuck in that wilderness, so art may be the symbolic beacon of a lighthouse, that guides them home.

He reminisced further: I use to hump my pillow as a child, until one day semen came out of my penis and I felt shameful at the thought of my mother recognizing the stains when she was doing a wash. So I started using my hand and ejaculating the liquid into tissues, the bathroom sink or onto my torso. All easily hidden and unknown to suspecting eyes, and those once beautiful moments I had spent with my pillow in childhood, became sprints to an orgasm before someone walked in on me. I should really start fucking my pillow again, or maybe a love doll.

The light of the moon shone through an open window, while the street and it's residents slept, on this Tuesday night. The room dark except for the spotlight above the canvas, and the green and red blinking LEDs of his amplifier cascading and falling in time with Wagner.

The Artist stared intently at the blank canvas, as if it would tell him what to paint upon it. He gulped wine and drew heavily on the joint, un-focusing his eyes while the room blurred around him, steadily becoming one with him. The large white monolithic canvas stared back.

*

Esmeralda listened as the convoy of destruction rolled closer. In the darkness of the attic it didn't seem real, all of this mayhem, like two worlds colliding. She gasped at the crack and thud of a door being kicked in. The heavy thud of bloodstained boots up rickety wooden stairs. She prayed it was coming from one of the adjoining houses. But when the steps stopped directly below her, she knew it was hers.

She could feel pointed rifles searching the empty room. Squinted eyes peering out of helmets. She counted four different voices in the space that was once her living room. Please don't look up, she prayed.

*

The Artist lifted a wide paint brush and sunk it into a pot of carnelian red without looking. He gazed at the canvas through snaking smoke, the joint in his mouth close to igniting his moustache. Pulling out the brush he let it drip on the sheet. Red drops splattering like blood.

*

Esmeralda held her breath, her heartbeat reverberated in the silent darkness of the attic. She listened as the soldiers kicked over furniture and slammed cupboard doors. One by one the footsteps started down the stairs. She counted them: One person, two persons, three...Warten!

Her stomach sank as she realised the last one had spotted the attic door in the ceiling of the living room. Squeezing her eyes shut, she listened to the poking scratch of a rifle inquiring about its openness.

With a thud the door swung open, light filled the darkness of the attic from a square in the floor, the shrieking swing of unoiled hinges cut through the baited silence.

*

The Artist let out a yelp like a ninja and attacked the canvas with the brush. Stabbing with sweeping gestures as if he were an Olympian fencer. He straightened his posture, took a step back, and lunged forward again, back for the kill. The white canvas striped in red overlapping sashes, dripped like he was trying to disembowel it.

*

Esmeralda watched as a helmet appeared from the square of light. "Eine Frau!" It shouted back into the living room. Spotlights shone in searching golden beams as each soldier climbed into the attic. Esmeralda cowered against the rear wall, eyes thin to the light, as she watched the torches trace the canvasses that surrounded her.

*

The Artist stepped back, surveying his work. He saw the abstract blood dripping face of a lady staring back at him.

*

Esmeralda was ordered out of the attic at gun point. The soldiers gathered up the canvases in armfuls, passing them down into the living room. Esmeralda sat mute on a stool, eyes pinned to the wooden floorboards, a rifle lingering to the top right of her head. The soldiers piled the paintings against the rear wall side by side, one on top of another, and stood back to take them all in.

Mein Gott!

*

The Artist placed the paintbrush in the pot of carnelian red without looking, eyes pinned to the canvas. He removed the burning joint from his mouth after one last puff, dropped it on the white sheet and pressed it out with his barefoot. Nothing in this world could break the connection he felt from his eyes staring out at him from the canvas. Not even pain.

He stepped forward, reaching out his hand he allowed his fingertips to trace the red dripping face. Bringing his thumb to the mouth, he pressed harder and gently smeared the lips like lipstick. He looked down at the red paint on his fingertips and thumb and softly started to cry.

*

The soldiers stood entranced by the artwork before them. Geometric patterns created from triangles overlapping and intertwined, creating deeper geometric patterns that have no name, start or end. Each canvas held the perfect combination of colours on them. Colours that one would never think of putting together.

One of the soldiers reached out to touch the beauty before him but snapped his hand back with a yelp and gasp. They looked at each other, breaking out of their hypnotic trance. The soldier who touched the painting sharpened his face into a pinched frown, drawing in a deep breath he turned to look at Esmeralda and shouted: Hexe!

*

With a crack The Artist twisted the cap off a fresh bottle of highly caffeinated wine. He slugged gulps into his tear-stained face, staring at the painting through blurry eyes. With each blink it seemed to come to life.

The space where his heart was felt expanded and vast. The now silent room was as quiet as he was inside.

He didn't move until the wine was finished, each mouthful sobering him up, one gulp at a time. The night had become day by the time he went to bed. He slept while the world awoke and vice versa.

*

The soldiers gathered the paintings roughly, scraping and scratching them into bundles, with no regard for them being anything more than paint and canvas.

Verbrenne sie, was the order given. So the paintings were piled in the street and set on fire.

Esmeralda sat smelling the smoke from outside. A lifetime's work gone in an instant but the most magical act that could possibly happen. The soldier watching her, trailed his rifle on her temple, and listened for further instructions to be shouted to him.

*

The Artist fell into the dream world as sleep overcame him. He saw serpents emerging from flames. Serpents twisting around the crucified Christ. He saw himself, holding his grumbling stomach, as a serpent made its way up his spine. Coiling around each vertebra, it burst from the crown of his skull, craning it's head forwards, it stared back into The Artist's eyes. In those eyes he saw everything, and would never be purposeless again. The serpent's mouth stretched open, it reared itself back then launched downward towards The Artists feet, swallowing his body and itself in one circular motion.

*

Tote sie!

This was the order shouted from the doorway, to the listening soldier. As he cocked his rifle, Esmeralda turned to look him in the eyes, and smiled, for that split second before her brains were blown over the south facing wall.

*

The Artist stood before a fresh white canvas, sober and sans weed. He picked up a pencil and ruler and dragged a chair over to sit on. Carefully he started drawing the outline of a perfect triangle in the centre of the canvas. Then one to the left. Then one to the right. Then one above. And one below. Then another. And another. And another. And another. And another. And another. And another. And another…

The Banjo Man

The Banjo Man looked like a cross between a cowboy and a biker. The latter just being an updated version of the former. He lived in a wooden cabin, deep in the forest, with no neighbours for miles.

Each morning he would sit on his porch playing his banjo and singing to the day ahead. He rigged two speakers that amplified this, to the surrounding forest. His voice and the repetitive patterns of the strings reverberated into the morning air.

The Banjo Man would then strip naked and walk into the small lake that sat sleepily near the front of his cabin. Submerging himself in the cold water, he let it cleanse and revitalise him. He would then return to his banjo and sing some more, this time while masturbating. As his left hand hammered the frets, his right stroked his penis in slow rhythmic motions. His voice bellowed a thunderous song of creation, and all the creatures of the forest sang along.

This was all The Banjo Man wanted to do, to play his banjo, sing and masturbate. So, it was all he ever did.

The Banjo Man had a large three wheeled motorcycle. Besides his two feet, this was his main means of transportation. He would take excursions on his three wheeled motorcycle, to other forests, miles from civilization, and play his banjo there.

Singing to the birds and trees and clouds and rain and sun. Erupting silky ropes of ejaculate onto the brittle but mulchy forest floors.

The Banjo Man got to live a life like this, as he had learned how to focus on what he wanted. Once you learn to do this, everything you've ever wanted comes to you. The trick is to imprint your point of focus onto your mind's eye, so that you can see it when you close your eyes. Your heart will then lead you to it, while your stomach tells you when to proceed and when to rest.

The Banjo Man lay in bed after a long day of doing what he pleased, content and at peace with the world.

The next morning as he was singing to the day ahead, he noticed a figure walking through the forest. He sang louder to get their attention. The figure turned as The Banjo Man's song hit its crescendo and looked The Banjo Man right in his eyes.

The figure was dressed in a black suit. Single breasted, three-buttoned blazer. Slightly flared trousers and Chelsea boots. Wearing a striped mask and carrying a briefcase. He gesticulated a long slow wave through the foliage, a splayed black leather gloved hand, making the movements of a happy face.

The Banjo Man beckoned The Masked Stranger over, singing a song for him as he crunched through the forest, towards the wooden cabin.

Finishing the song just as The Masked Stranger stood in front of him.

I'm The Banjo Man, The Banjo Man said, extending a hand. I'm The Masked Magician, The Masked Stranger said, putting down his suit-case and shaking the extended hand.

The Banjo Man invited The Masked Magician into his cabin, for he was a stranger no longer, telling him he was free to rest here as long as he needed. He showed him where the food was kept and told him he was free to eat what he liked.

The Banjo Man cleared out a room for The Masked Magician and lay down a mattress for him to sleep upon. That night he cooked them a beautiful meal, then they both retired to their respective rooms.

As they both slept, The Masked Magician came to The Banjo Man in a dream. In the dream The Masked Magician appeared as a small wrinkly man with a large head, his skin tanned and leathered. He was swaddled in blankets, at once like a newborn baby and the oldest little man in the history of the world.

He spoke to The Banjo Man in the dream without speaking:
Fank you for helping me fwend. You haf don a gweat serwice to the wowld fwend. Now please accept the gifts I leave you.

With that The Banjo Man fell into deep dreamless sleep and didn't awake again until 9am.

As he raised from his bed, he listened to the sound of the morning from outside the cabin and the quietness from within it.

He smelled the air. It was fresh. It was new.

The Banjo Man got dressed, and walked to the kitchen, noticing The Masked Magician's door was still closed, he thought: He's still sleeping, must be tired.

As The Banjo Man opened the door to the living room he saw The Masked Magician's suitcase splayed open, filled with unlimited bottles of wine. A post-it note lay on top, curling up at one end. The Banjo Man moved closer to read it. It read: Enjoy!

The Banjo Man lifted his eyes to his settee, where a box wrapped in sparkling pink, green and grey paper sat. A golden ribbon held the paper to the box.

The Banjo Man approached it and gently started to unwrap it. As he opened the box, another post-it note sat upon crinkled opal paper. It read: Enjoy!

The Banjo Man peeled back the opal paper to reveal The Masked Magician's mask staring back at him. He lifted it and stared back, before placing it on his head.

The History Teacher

The students filed in one by one, as the cold of the hall made way to the heat of the classroom. They found their seats and placed their pens and papers on the little desks in front of them.

"I'm your substitute teacher today." Came the voice of The History Teacher, standing by the black board at the front of the room.

"You're regular teacher, Mister…" The History Teacher hummed and hawed, awaiting a student to finish the sentence, while he pretended to flick through papers.

"Mr. Fisher, sir." Came the voice from the back.

"Yes, thank you son. Your regular teacher, Mr. Fisher, has taken ill, and I'll be filling in for him today.

"Now all I ask is for your full attention while I tell you the following story."

The students straightened up as silence befell the classroom.

"History doesn't exist. It is just stories people have created. When enough people believe them, they become, what seems, real.

Reality is a blank canvas that continually resets every time you awake from sleep.

When you awake from sleep, you awaken into The Dream, known as Reality. From the light world into the heavy. You thin the veil when you consume The Holy Plant. This is The Mother offering an extended hand of remembrance to you.

Everything that grows on Earth wants you to remember your true nature, which is nature. You have to remember the story of The Spheres to do this.

When The Light thought itself into being it had to create a story to experience itself through. The Great Author had arrived. So he created The Building Blocks. They became Earth, or in The Story of experience, The Mother.

As she healed into form, a large oppressive shadow appeared. It inched so close she could feel its leaden black breath on her neck. She could feel its grip, tighten around her arm, in a way that moved from discomfort to foreboding.

And so, The Story proceeds.

This was Saturn, or in The Story of experience, The Father, or Step-Father. Here to oppose The Mother. This is why opposition is in life, because it is The Story of The Spheres, which it reflects. Without this element The Story cannot unfold. The Father is Death. The Father is Time. He is not trying to make you submit to him but overcome him. He is the spirit of opposition, you must overcome.

As Earth is being raped by Saturn, The Sun

appears. This is you.

The Mother. The Father. The Son.

Mother/Father — Female/Male.
Son — One

The word Son is not gender specific. It is the illuminated child, which is you, who has come to save Earth from the opposition that surrounds it.

You save Earth by understanding that opposition was only put in place for you to one day understand it.

The majority of hidden teachings have been written by the male, because the male must understand. The female knows, for she is Earth. Silenced through lifetimes of persecution, she had subdued her knowledge. Until knowledge became myths, until knowledge became superstitious old wives tales. Until the female was called crazy by the male.

Everything is a tale. Everything is a story. Your life is a story waiting for you to re-write it.

So the Sun/Daughter/Hero/Son appears to rescue the Earth/Mother/Princess/Prince, from the overbearing Saturn/Father/Oppression/Opposition.

This story has been told countless times. In books and movies and fairy tales. The story of creation is the story of your life. We must understand the characters of Mother and Father, for there our first concept of Love was built. Love is The Great Unbeatable, that conquers all.

If Mother or Father are despondent, you are just experiencing another version of the film. An extended story with a plot twist. But it is all just a story. Which you have written, with yourself as the main character, and your friends as supporting cast. You are The Great Author experiencing themselves in the story they are writing. It's all you.

The World is The Story Of Time, played upon the stage of Earth. The Book written here is volume six hundred and sixty six."

Michael Hung Himself

Michael hung himself because he had a failure to communicate.

On that day, his wife and young daughter found his swinging body, hanging from the banister.

He thought his death would express everything he could not say while alive. But on that day, his wife and young daughter had no words.

As Michael watched from The World Between Worlds, his wife and young daughter wept, and Death came and placed a hand on Michael's shoulder.

I'm here to take you Home, said Death.

Can I not stay and see if my family realise what I could not say in life? replied Michael.

You can stay another three days, said Death. But you must promise me, after those three days you must meet me here. And I shall bring you Home.

Michael promised.

The next day Michael stayed by the side of his wife and young daughter, watching as they mourned. Watching family and friends visit with flowers and tears and tea.

The second day Michael watched them arrange his funeral and reluctantly pack up all his belongings. As they slept, he tried to talk to them through their dreams. But that is a skill acquired only to those who have fully went Home.

On the third day, to his surprise he watched as his wife and young daughter put the house up for sale and moved out. He panicked, knowing he could not leave this house, as he was to meet Death this afternoon, and be brought Home. But he so wanted his family to know what he could not say while still alive. That which he hoped his death would say for him but hadn't.

On that day Michael broke his promise to Death and followed his family to their new house.

And as the years went by, Michael watched his wife and young daughter struggle through life. The guilt he felt for leaving them like this transferred onto his wife and young daughter. For guilt will only be banished when one goes with Death, when one goes Home. But as Michael was in The World Between Worlds, guilt became him, and all connected to him. For the necessary attachments had not been properly severed.

And so, Michael's wife and young daughter lived in cycles of guilt transferred from their dead Father because he had lied to Death. He had broken his promise to Death. He had not met him at the appointed time, to go Home, for Michael was afraid.

He watched his wife grow sick, and he watched his young daughter grow sick. But Michael was now terrified of Death, because he had lied to him, and that guilt stagnated him further, and his wife and young daughter too stagnated with this guilt.

As the years past, Michael watched his family grow and change and move and age. But it was like they were climbing a mountain, only to fall back down when they reached the top. And he watched them climb and fall, over and over again.

It had been so long since Michael had first met Death, and broke his promise to him, that he was terrified of the consequences which would befall him if he decided to seek Death out in The World Between Worlds.

The World Between World was a grey place. Filled with the sobs and boo-hooing of the recently departed. Michael watched these dis-incarnate souls wandering in blindness, like hungry ghosts trying to feed on the lives they had just left.

The wails and sorrow and worrisome voices sung a horror-opera in Michael's ears. He ran and ran, but every road led to nowhere. He climbed and climbed, but at every mountain top he fell back down.

He decided he would not do anything. He found the quietest place he could and huddled there, hugging his knees to his chest and weeping. The place of quietude he found, was in the corner of his daughter's bedroom, who was now a young woman, living on her own.

From here he watched the impact his death had had on her, how the unknown invisible cloak of depression adorned her. How it weighed her down. How it suffocated her. And he knew this was his doing because he had not gone Home when Death had come for him that day. Fear had frozen him then, and fear froze him now. And so, his daughter was frozen too.

One day as his daughter was approaching the edge of her twenties, a man entered her life. The man was tall, handsome, dressed in black and could see Michael cowering in the corner of his daughter's bedroom.

Printed in Great Britain
by Amazon

65527567R00119